THE DARK DAYS OF SPRING

THE DARK DAYS OF SPRING

Smugglers' Cottage was a haven for Lynda, the perfect place to rest and recuperate. She came with high hopes to the Devonshire village only to find that peace, even here, was hard to find. The assorted members of the Hathersage family; the past and present; the natural and spectral—all combined to disturb the early spring. Even Adam Taylor, the young doctor to whom Lynda was attracted, had secrets. Then tragedy visited the cottage...

The Dark Days Of Spring

by

Mary Mackie

Dales Large Print Books
Long Preston, North Yorkshire,
England.

British Library Cataloguing in Publication Data.

Mackie, Mary
The dark days of spring.

A catalogue record for this book is available from the British Library

ISBN 1-85389-608-X pbk

First published in Great Britain by Robert Hale & Company, 1974

Published in Large Print October, 1996 by arrangement with R.M. Mackie.

Dales Large Print is an imprint of
Library Magna Books Ltd.
Printed and bound in Great Britain by
T.J. Press (Padstow) Ltd., Cornwall, PL28 8RW.

For Mum and Dad
with thanks for everything.

CHAPTER ONE

I woke up feeling groggy—the effects of sleeping tablets—and it took me a few minutes to register the fact that I was in the small bedroom of Gran's cottage, and that the scratching on the door was her Cairn terrier, Smokey, trying to attract my attention. Rolling dizzily out of bed, I opened the door and let the little dog in. He ran around me a couple of times and then leapt onto the bed, settling down comfortably in the warm place I had just vacated.

The smell of frying bacon which was finding its way from the kitchen below made my stomach start working. Calling to Gran that I was on my way, I washed and dressed hurriedly.

From the window at the top of the dark stairs I could see the winter-bare gardens, the apple trees and unkempt grass, with the straggling copse nicknamed The Wilderness stretching beyond. The view was blurred through the driving sleet that was falling, pouring off the sloping glass roof of the conservatory built onto the back of the cottage, and I shivered as I turned to go down the narrow stairs, bending my head to avoid the low black beam half-way down.

It was a relief to sit by the blazing fire in the sitting-room, where Gran had set the table for breakfast. And soon, with food in my stomach and Smokey curled warmly at my feet, I began to feel more human.

Gran sat opposite me, watching me gravely. She was short and plump, with grey hair cut short around her apple-cheeked face, and I knew she was worried about me. I had run to her for comfort when my world disintegrated around me. She would give me what I needed most—loving care—without asking too many questions. I was glad of that, for I would be too ashamed to tell her the whole truth.

'You'm not looking well, m'dear,' she said worriedly. 'They sent you out too soon from that hospital.'

'It's not that,' I assured her. 'It's just the effects of the journey, and the sleeping tablets. I always feel woozy first thing in the morning.'

‘Still taking they tablets, then?’ she said, with a frown which conveyed her dislike of all ‘new-fangled’ medicines.

‘Yes, but I shall begin to tail them off now. The bottle I’ve got will be the last. I don’t want to get addicted.’

‘No, indeed you don’t. There be enough of that sort of thing, so I hear. You’ll sleep all right, with the sea air and everything. A good holiday and a lot of looking-after be what you need.’

She poured me another cup of her hot, strong tea and added two spoonsful of sugar, which would have horrified me a year ago, when I was watching my waistline. But that was back in the time when life had been running smoothly. The time before Richard. Before the accident and the months in hospital. Before I turned into a walking skeleton twitching with neuroses.

‘Not that ’tis the best time of year,’ Gran added, looking out of the cottage window at the mixture of rain and snow that was still steadily coming down. ‘But you’ve no call to stir. Baker van calls, and the butcher and grocer. Us won’t starve, nor freeze. There’s a good stack of logs in the shed, and plenty of coal. And, please

God, the winter won't last much longer. 'Tis March come Saturday, and there be snowdrops in the churchyard.'

It was comfortable here in the main room of the cottage, with the fire in the corner grate and all around me objects which I remembered from childhood summers spent with Gran. The front door opened directly into this room. The stairs led up from the corner by the front door and the tiny kitchen at the back was reached by two more steps. That was all there was to the ground floor, apart from the conservatory built onto the kitchen.

On a day such as this, the cottage interior was dark, but too well known to feel gloomy. I could have been content to stay here in the dim warmth for ever, but I had a feeling there was something Freudian about it—a return to the womb, or something—and I had to stop myself from giving in to it.

'I think I might go up to the Mount today,' I said. 'They'll think it's funny if I don't even call in to see them.'

'P'raps so,' Gran replied dubiously. 'But you won't go unless this weather clears. Don't want you catchin' cold on top of everything else. Maybe Melly will call here.

I told her you was comin'.'

And that, I thought, would suit Gran. If she had her way, I would never visit Hathercombe Mount. It was an old, old jealousy based on a total misunderstanding, but no one could convince Gran of that. She was certain that the Hathersages had thought her son unworthy to marry their beautiful daughter. The Hathersages were the local gentry, while the Fieldings were poor villagers.

But Gran was entirely wrong. My mother's family might live in a great rambling house and have generations of traceable history, but they had to fight for every penny, whereas my father had been a brilliant architect whose services were much in demand. He had been able to provide mother with things she had only dreamed about, and the Hathersages had been only too happy for her. But Gran couldn't believe it, immersed too deeply in her own sense of inferiority, and she was jealous of my feelings for the Hathersages, especially now that my parents were dead—in an air crash in Italy. My brother and I were all Gran had left of her only son, and she wasn't too keen on sharing us with mother's family.

'Melly wrote to me several times while I was in hospital,' I said. 'But she always manages to write reams and not really say anything.'

'She be a dear child,' Gran said warmly, pouring out more cups of tea from the big brown pot. 'The best of the lot, though 'tis not my place to say so. Poor child, her do lead a dog's life with all they others puttin' on her. Bain't no more'n a skivvy.'

'I thought they had a housekeeper?'

'So they do. But the place be that big and now that other woman there. Bess Porter do say as how she don't lift a finger to help, though she be a great one at giving orders.'

I gathered that she was referring to my Uncle James' recently-acquired second wife. My cousin Melissa—known as Melly—had written briefly about it, but she hadn't said how she felt about her new step-mother.

'What's she like?' I asked. 'She's foreign, isn't she?'

'So they say. I ain't seen her myself, but Bess Porter don't think much to her. Of course, she be powerful rich. May I be forgiven for saying so, but I reckon that's why James married her.'

'What about her son? Melly's letters were full of him.'

Gran made a derogatory sound in her throat. 'I only know what Bess Porter say and that ain't anything good. Seems like this Guy ain't much more'n a playboy... But I can't sit talkin' all day. Must get these dishes washed... No, you sit still. I can manage.'

* * * *

The weather cleared after a while, though there was still a brisk cold wind and Gran thought my coat wasn't half warm enough. Before she let me venture out, she insisted that I wear a big woolly scarf round my head and tucked inside my collar. I adjusted it while looking in the mirror at the foot of the stairs, in the grey light coming from the window up on the small square landing, and the sight of my reflection depressed me. My eyes looked unnaturally large, great hollows above thin cheeks, and the gold of my hair was dulled. I tucked it carefully inside the scarf, making sure that the swathe down the left side covered the jagged red scar which ran from my forehead to above my ear. There was not much trace of the healthy female of last summer, when I had been deeply tanned, long hair shining and queer tawny eyes bright with joy. Golden girl, Richard had called me. Handsome, laughing, carefree Richard, who had betrayed me so utterly, so thoughtlessly. I wondered what he would feel if he saw me now. Remorse, perhaps? Pity? But no. It would never occur to Richard that he might be to blame, in part, for my present state.

It would have been so easy for me to change my mind about going out, easier by far to stay here in the cottage, curled up by the fire with a book. But I had been warned against that by my doctor. I had to get out and meet people, begin to live a normal life again.

The cottage lay half a mile from the village centre, on a tree-lined road with tall hedges. Our immediate neighbour towards the village was a tiny Norman church with a squat tower, surrounded by a churchyard edged with dark yews. On the other side lay the long driveway to Hathercombe Manor, gateless posts flanking the entrance, and beyond it the recently-built Garden Centre enclosed by tall yellow walls.

It was four years since I had visited

Hathercombe, so I had not seen the Garden Centre before, but knew it to be the brainchild of my Uncle James. For years the Hathersages had made outdoor furniture, providing work for a good few villagers, and the success of their garden benches and tables had prompted the beginning of the ambitious Garden Centre, where the furniture could be sold along with all the other paraphernalia of the modern garden. It was yet another attempt to make money for the great gaunt monster of Hathersage Mount, which devoured pounds and pence effortlessly, and ceaselessly.

The drive was muddy and rutted. For as long as I could remember they had talked about putting down gravel or tarmac, but there was always something more urgent needed. The old house demanded constant repairs and renovations, so the drive stayed muddy and I walked along the wet verge, wishing I had some wellingtons instead of fashion boots.

On my left, at the end of Gran's garden, the apple trees were bare, their branches being whipped by the fierce wind. Beyond the fence at the bottom, The Wilderness was a tangle of trees and bushes, the ground uneven and marked by outcrops of rock. The drive climbed up, past the trees and the yellow wall on the other side, then, as I reached the top of the rise, the combe spread out before me, sage green grass and patches of black, dead heather and gorse bushes. From here I could see the Mount, a grey structure all corners and irregularities, built mainly around three sides of a cobbled yard. The drive divided, the left hand stretch running to the terraced front of the house, which looked out over the cliff top to the sea, but I took the right fork, which brought me to the stable-yard and the ivy-clad walls of the rear of the house.

The end of one wing was still used as stables for the ponies which my cousin Martin kept. He gave riding lessons and in summer arranged pony-treks for the tourists. It appeared that he had just been putting the horses in the paddock, for I could see them running inside the fence, and as I approached the house Martin himself came round the corner behind me, whistling. He was dressed in old slacks and a thick polo-neck sweater, a sturdy young man with a ruddy, tanned face and curly brown hair tousled by the wind.

Seeing me, he came across the cobbles

and stopped a few few feet away, his even white teeth showing in a grin as he recognised me.

'Lynda! I heard you were coming. How are you?'

'Fine, thanks! And you?'

'Oh, I'm the healthy type.' He looked me up and down, frowning. 'You're awfully thin. I thought you were supposed to be better.'

'I am, more or less. And you, I notice, are as charming as ever.'

Martin laughed and took my arm. 'Better come inside before this wind blows you away.'

He took me through the kitchen, where I re-met the housekeeper Mrs Porter—the Bess Porter from whom Gran gleaned all her information—and on into the corridor which emerged at one side of the curving, Y-shaped staircase in the freezing spaces of the great hall. And it was here that I heard the hammerings and bangings which reverberated around the house.

'We're having central heating put in,' Martin explained as we crossed the cold stone floor. 'Gas-fired, which is the most efficient, according to Lottie. But since she's paying for it...'

'Your step-mother is?' I queried.

Martin paused, pulling a wry face. 'Well, *we* couldn't afford it. And she's always complaining how cold the place is, so she offered to have heating put in.'

I wanted to ask him what this Lottie was like, what he thought of her, but we had reached the sitting-room door which Martin opened and ushered me inside. It was a long room with four tall windows looking seawards, half a dozen armchairs, various tables, and a long settee placed squarely in front of a roaring log fire where a dark-haired woman was busy with what looked like accounts ledgers. She glanced up as Martin and I went in and I was struck by her beauty, perfect features and warm olive skin set off by dark, lustrous eyes.

'Oh, Lottie,' said Martin. 'This is my cousin Lynda. She's staying at Smuggler's Cottage with her grandmother.'

Lottie smiled warmly at me. 'Of course. I have heard about you, Lynda. My husband's sister ran off to marry the talented local boy, and you are the result. So romantic.'

'They didn't exactly run away,' I said defensively. 'Mother's family were as pleased about it as anyone.'

'And she isn't the only result,' Martin said. 'She's got a brother, too.' He turned to me. 'How is Bob? Still looking for oil?'

I nodded. 'In the Persian Gulf, as far as I know. He isn't much on letter-writing.'

It was hot in front of the fire and I threw back my scarf, smoothing my hair carefully to avoid displaying the scar left by my accident.

'Have you seen Melly?' Martin asked of his step-mother.

She had returned her attention to the accounts and looked up vaguely. 'Oh...yes. She went upstairs with the doctor. He came to see Aunt Maude. I don't wish to appear rude, Martin, but I have to get on with this work and the workmen are fixing the radiators in the office. I'd be grateful if I could have some privacy.'

I saw Martin bristle and his mouth tighten as he glanced at me. 'We'll make ourselves scarce, Lyn. I'm sure Melly will be glad to see you.'

Leaving the room, he closed the door with a bang.

'You don't like her much, do you?' I said.

'No, but Dad seems happy enough, and she does seem ready to put her money to good use.'

'She's younger than I expected.'

Martin grunted, looking at me with a glint in his eye. 'She's older than she looks. I don't know exactly how much, but Guy must be nearly thirty so she can't be much less than fifty. Of course, she can afford to take good care of her looks... The whole thing came as a bit of a shock to us. Dad started taking regular trips to London and one day he told us that on the next trip he'd be getting married. We didn't have much say on the subject. So Lottie arrived and a few days later Guy turned up. And here we are, one big happy family.'

'Except that *you* aren't happy,' I commented. 'Is Melly?'

'My dear little sister,' Martin said dryly, 'is over the moon with joy. And when you meet Guy you'll understand why. Come on, let's go and find her. And if Adam's still here you can get re-acquainted with him.'

'I've been expecting to run into him,' I said as we climbed the wide stairway. 'He's Gran's doctor now, isn't he? She talks very favourably about him. It seems funny. I remember him as a great lanky boy, all arms and legs, and bright red hair. It must be...oh, ten years since I last saw him, but that was only a brief glimpse. I'll never forget the day the two of you had that fight. I never saw so much blood.'

At the landing where the stairs divided, Martin paused to grin at me. 'That was entirely my fault. I was teasing Jenny—you remember how scared she was of heights—I tried to get her near the cliff and Adam rushed to her defence. Surprised me a bit. I never thought he had it in him.'

'Is Jenny still in America?' I asked. 'Melly never mentioned her in her letters.'

'She wouldn't. We're all a bit disgusted with dear cousin Jenny. The way she went off like that. Uncle Jonathon gets an occasional letter from her and he doesn't seem to mind too much. But it wasn't fair of her to go so far away. She's all he's got. He doted on that girl, turned her into a spoiled bitch. But now he seems proud of her success. She's made quite a name for herself, if you count being a model as something to be proud of.'

Taking the left-hand branch of the stairs, we made our way along the dim, twisty corridors. My mind was full of memories of childhood summers when my brother had been off camping and Youth Hostelling and I had come to stay with Gran and play with my three cousins; Martin, Melissa and beautiful silver-blonde Jenny, whose fairy-like grace and charm had woven spells around everyone, with the exception of Martin, who had no imagination. Perhaps he was right and she had been spoiled. Certainly she always managed to have her own way. But I don't remember anyone resenting the fact. Jenny was...just Jenny. I always wished that I could be like her.

A suite of three rooms at the end of the South wing was inhabited by my great-aunt Maude, who had lived in her private world here for forty years. She was a very old lady now, nearing ninety, and when Martin knocked on the door I was astonished to hear a key turn inside.

My cousin Melissa stood there, poor old Melly, unlovely and unloved. She was short and fat, her hair thick with grease and her white face scarred and erupting with acne. At seventeen this had seemed a passing phase, but Melly was twenty-one now and I was appalled to see that she hadn't changed. She would have been repulsive if she weren't so desperately affectionate, like a great ugly puppy, and now she threw herself at me and hugged me.

'Lyn! Oh, Lyn! How lovely to see you. Are you all right? Oh, you do look pale. And thin!'

'You might ask her how she managed that,' Martin said darkly, glancing significantly at his sister's plump figure in the baggy skirt and jumper. 'Give her a few hints, Lynda.'

Melly's great brown eyes grew wide with pain and her full mouth trembled, making me sigh inwardly to think that the life-long feud between them was still continuing.

'We can't all be as perfect as you are,' I said tartly, and Martin laughed and said it was clear my tongue hadn't got any sweeter.

He went away, leaving Melly and I alone in the cluttered room filled with ugly Victorian furniture, lace doilies on every flat space supporting Aunt Maude's vast collection of fragile ornaments.

'I *am* dieting,' Melly said in a small voice. 'It just doesn't seem to do much good. I don't enjoy being fat.'

'You shouldn't let Martin bother you,' I said. 'Melly, why was the door locked?'

'Oh, it needn't have been,' she replied, 'not with us in here. But, you see, Aunt Maude took to roaming about the house and once she almost fell down the stairs, so we have to lock her in. She's got an electric bell she can ring if she wants us, and we never leave her alone for long, and there's everything she needs in this suite, even a bathroom.'

'I see,' I said, feeling sorry for the old lady who was virtually a prisoner. 'And what does she say to the central heating? That must be a bit of an upheaval.'

'It is,' my cousin said, 'but we've decided to leave Aunt Maude's rooms for the time being. There'd be too much noise and dirt. She's going to have her fires, as usual, and...' She broke off as the far door opened and a tall, red-headed man came from the bedroom.

Dr Adam Taylor was an angular man with long limbs and square shoulders, a bony face still covered in the freckles he had hated as a boy, but his hair had toned down to a rich chestnut and he had lost the gawkiness of the young medical student he had been when last I saw him.

Melly smiled archly at him. 'I bet you don't know who this is.'

'Then you lose,' he said, with a smile which briefly dispelled the serious look on his face. 'This is Lynda Fielding. Has to be. How are you, Lynda?' He switched the black case to his left hand and held out his right.

'I'm fine, thank you,' I said. 'How are you? And how is Aunt Maude?'

'About how you'd expect an old lady of her age to be. Are you going in to see her?'

'I thought I would. Will it be all right?'

'It will for her, but you should be prepared. She's lost all sense of time. Usually she takes me for my father. So don't expect her to know who you are.'

But great-aunt Maude had always been vague, her mind wandering in strange channels, so I went into the bedroom with no trepidation. It was hot in there, the room feeling stuffy after the coldness of the rest of the house. A bright fire blazed in the grate, with a guard locked all around it. Above the bedhead, gauzy curtains framed the picture of a bone-china-fragile old lady. Pink face, bright blue eyes and a cloud of thin white hair. It was only when one came closer that the network of lines on her face was visible, like crazing in the glaze of old pottery, and one saw the trembling of the dried-up hands on the coverlet.

She was looking at me alertly and before I could speak her voice rang out with surprising strength. 'Now, Nora, don't come fussing round me. Where have you left that brat? I hope he isn't running loose in my sitting-room, breaking all my things. I'll never forgive him for what he did last time. That little tea-pot was priceless to me. So keep your Martin out of my rooms, do you hear?'

'Aunt Maude,' I said softly. 'It's Lynda. Lynda Fielding. Julia's daughter.'

'Julia?' The old lady peered at me, making a kind of clucking noise, and her hands moved restlessly. 'It's only right. Don't let them stop you. You're a lucky girl.' Her eyes were suddenly full of tears. 'He might have married me, but times were different then. I might have had a son like that. No, no. Don't fuss me, Julia. I'm only a silly old woman.'

I had bent over her, worried by her agitation, but as I did so she relaxed and smiled tremulously up at me. 'You're a sweet girl, Julia. Come back and see me tomorrow. I'm going to sleep now.'

I backed out of the room, feeling

dazed, and closed the door softly to find Melly and Adam Taylor watching me expectantly.

'How long has she been like that?' I asked.

'She's been deteriorating slowly over the years,' the young doctor said gravely. 'Did she know you?'

'No. My name meant nothing to her. She...' To my consternation, my head began to whirl and a mist crept before my eyes. The brisk walk and the sudden changes of temperature... I was hardly aware of Adam putting me into a chair and forcing my head down between my knees, his cool fingers massaging my neck.

Then Melly was there with a glass of water which revived me so that I was able to sit up and apologise. Adam Taylor knelt before me, looking stern and professional.

'You should never have turned out on a day like this,' he said. 'What time did you arrive last night?'

'I don't know exactly. After eleven. But I'm all right, and I was warned not to let myself become a recluse.'

'That's all very well,' he replied. 'But there's no point in overdoing things. You walked up here in that wind when you ought to have taken a day or two to recuperate from the journey. Come with me now. I'll give you a lift home.'

CHAPTER TWO

For several days I was cushioned and cosseted. Every time I tried to help with the work Gran told me sternly that Dr Taylor had left strict instructions that I was to rest. It seemed to make no difference to her that Adam Taylor was not my doctor. He was hers, and that was all she cared. So I sat about and read books which Melly brought and even made a start on the novel I had always wanted to write, while outside the cottage March arrived with high winds and lashing rain.

Melly's conversation when she visited me revolved, as her last few letters had done, around her new step-brother. It was a case of "Guy says..." and "Guy did..." and "When Guy..." so that I became increasingly curious to meet this paragon. Now I understood Martin's enigmatic remark. Obviously Melly was very taken by Guy.

During this time of quiet, Smokey was my constant companion. He was getting on in years and loved to lie curled up at my feet on the hearthrug, or, when he could manage it, snuggle beside me on the settee. But when Melly appeared he always retreated to the kitchen. She was too fussily affectionate for Smokey's taste, being so desperate for friendship that she was apt to smother anyone, and anything, she liked. It made me wonder whether the unknown Guy was subjected to the same treatment.

On the first really fine day we had had since my arrival in Hathercombe, Gran and I walked the short distance to the Garden Centre to buy a pot-plant to replace one which had died. There was a car park behind the yellow wall and beyond it a bank of budding daffodils with some steps leading to the prefabricated shop. Greenhouses lay to one side and behind them a wide paved area where garden furniture, statues, birdbaths etc. were on display. While Gran wandered round the greenhouses, I strolled among the hardware, noting that, besides the sturdy Hathersage furniture, they were also selling the cheaper type, plastic and tubular steel.

The gardens stretched away beyond—neat rows of plants and small trees all labelled—and there were three gardeners at work on a patch of bare soil, but there were few customers. I wondered whether the Garden Centre had proved to be the success for which my Uncle James had hoped.

And then I saw both of my uncles, James and Jonathon, emerging from the shop. Before I could reach them, Uncle James had turned away towards the car park, a mountain of a man with a vast stomach and thinning hair. Uncle Jonathon was smaller, and bent from years of working at a craftsman's bench in the furniture factory.

'Uncle Jonathon!' I called, but he walked on, with the swaying limp caused by an accident in his youth. Then I remembered that he was stone deaf, so I ran after him and tapped his arm.

His warm smile in that brown, gnome-like face was always a joy to see and now it beamed out as he grabbed me by the shoulders.

'Lynda! Are you better? I've been wanting to come and see you, but your Gran disapproves of me for some reason so I thought it best to stay away.'

His voice was quiet, as in most deaf people, and I remembered to enunciate clearly so that he could lip-read.

'You should have come. Gran won't eat you. Are you all right?'

'Never better. We've just been negotiating a deal for some park benches for Barnstaple Corporation. When are you coming up to the Mount?'

'As soon as I can.'

Uncle Jonathon smiled and nodded. 'Melly tells me you're writing a book.'

'I'm trying to,' I admitted. 'Have you still got all those notes and things about the family?'

'Oh, yes. Is that what the book's about? You're welcome to come and see the papers any time.'

'I might do that,' I said. 'But I thought you were saving them for Jenny.'

At the mention of his daughter's name a shadow crossed his face. 'No,' he said sadly. 'Not now. I hoped Jenny would take over my interest in the Mount and family history, but it always bored her. And now she's gone away. Nobody else is interested. So if you can make use of my notes I'll be glad. You might write us a brochure for the hotel.'

'What hotel?' I asked blankly, but at that moment Gran appeared, plant-pot in hand, and Uncle Jonathon only stayed long enough to wish her 'Good morning' before making excuses about work to do.

* * * *

As we walked back to the cottage I was about to ask Gran whether she knew anything about a hotel when we paused to allow a car to emerge from the driveway to the Mount. It was a dark blue Viva, Dr Taylor's car, and when he saw us he stopped and climbed out.

'Nice to see you out again, Miss Fielding,' he greeted. 'How are you feeling now?'

'Is that a professional enquiry?' I asked, and Gran said, 'Lynda!' in a disapproving tone, adding to the red-headed doctor, 'She be a lot better, I'm glad to say. But this be her first time out since she fainted.'

'I didn't faint!' I protested.

'No, well it's hardly been the weather to tempt one into long walks,' Adam Taylor said conversationally. 'Actually, I stopped to ask if you were well enough to do me a favour.'

'Anything short of a cross-country run,' I said recklessly.

'Then how about having dinner with me tonight?'

Surprise left me momentarily speechless and while I struggled for words Gran spoke for me. 'Why, doctor, you'm a genius. That be what she needs. A proper night out. Do her the world of good.'

'I thought you said it was a favour,' I said suspiciously. 'It sounds more like a prescription.'

'No, I assure you. It will save me from a boring evening. My father's having some friends in to play bridge and I'd rather not be there.'

It wasn't the most flattering offer I had ever received, but I agreed to go.

'There must have been somebody else he could ask,' I said to Gran as we went through the cottage gate and were greeted noisily by Smokey.

'Maybe there be, but I don't know of any. They do say he don't take much to women. Least, not since Jenny Hathersage went away.'

'Jenny?' Instantly I was all ears. 'Why, was he keen on her?'

'Oh, I don't know. 'Twas all gossip. Both of them away in Lonnon—him at the hospital doin' his trainin' and her workin' for the magazines. Most like they never even met. Lunnon be a big place. And I don't remember Adam Taylor ever bein' the kind of boy that chased girls. They do say he be a confined bachelor, but 'tis his business, not mine.'

I think she meant "confirmed" bachelor, but I kept my smile to myself.

* * * *

That evening, as Adam Taylor and I drove towards Ilfracombe, I was tense and edgy, wishing that I had not agreed to come. And Adam's silence seemed to indicate that he, too, had misgivings about what I was sure was a charitable effort to bring me out of my shell.

We arrived at the best hotel in the town, where he had booked a table, and a glance in the mirror in the foyer confirmed my bitter feelings that I was an object of pity. The blue woollen dress seemed to emphasise my skinniness and the one whisky-coloured eye which was visible glared balefully from its hollow in my face. Nervously, I stroked the curtain of hair across the left side of my face and preceded my escort into the dining-room.

I don't remember what we talked about for the first half hour or so, but I recall Adam visibly relaxing as the sherry and soup were dealt with. It made me stop worrying about myself and begin to wonder why he looked so strained and why his smile was so rare.

Halfway through the main course, he leaned forward and said casually. 'Would you like to tell me about the accident?'

'Therapy?' I demanded.

'Interest. Curiosity, if you like. All I know is that you were in a car crash. Truly, Lynda...' He paused, watching my hand, which had begun its habitual stroking of my hair. I was so acutely conscious of that livid scar that my hand worked of its own accord, like a nervous tic.

I forced myself to stop it, picked up my fork. 'There isn't much more to tell. I was lucky to come out of it alive, though at first I didn't see it that way.'

'Were you driving?'

'No. I was with...with a friend. It was foggy and we were going round this big roundabout when a lorry appeared from a side turning, going like a bat out of hell, and crunched into us.

'Was your friend hurt?'

'Cuts and bruises. They didn't even keep him in hospital.'

'So you got the full force of it.'

'Yes.' My hand crept up again, to make sure the curtain was in place.

'You'll have to break yourself of that habit,' Adam Taylor said quietly. 'That scar *will* fade, and...'

His voice tailed off as my face flamed with horror and embarrassment. How did he know? When had he seen...?

'You almost fainted in my arms,' he said. 'And scars don't worry me. I've seen a great deal worse in my time. You ought to see the one I've got.'

'Where?' I demanded.

A twinkle appeared in eyes that I suddenly noticed were a clear green. 'Ask me again when we know each other better. But you were telling me...about the accident.'

'I've told you all I remember. You don't

want to hear about my months in hospital, I'm sure. And don't you get tired of people talking about their illnesses?'

'Um, yes, I do rather. Except when I'm on duty, of course. How long will you be staying in Hathercombe?'

'I don't know. I might decide to stay and find a job, if Gran will have me.'

'Won't your boy-friend miss you?'

I looked across the table at him, meeting his enquiring glaze blankly. 'What boy-friend?'

'Why, the...the one who...the driver of the car.'

'I haven't seen or heard from him since the night of the crash,' I said levelly. 'And I'd rather not talk about it, if you don't mind.'

His freckled face clouded with sympathy. 'I'm sorry, Lynda. If I had realised...'

'It doesn't matter. I'm well rid of him and I know that now. Can't we talk about you for a change?'

'Not much to talk about. I'm a doctor. Group practice in Ilfracombe. What else is there to say?'

I longed to ask him about Jenny, beautiful, ethereal cousin Jenny. Had he been in love with her once? But one didn't ask questions like that, not on so short an acquaintance.

'It's funny,' I mused. 'When I first saw you, I assumed you would be married. Somehow I always imagine GPs as married.'

'Most of them are,' Adam said, and picked up the menu. 'What would you like for dessert?'

After the meal, we moved into the bar, where couples were dancing in a dimly-lit alcove to taped music. Adam led me to join the dancers, holding me in a grip that was firm but impersonal.

'What was your real motive for asking me out tonight?' I asked.

'Loneliness.'

I looked up into his face. 'Yours, or mine?'

'Mine,' he said. 'Does that surprise you?'

'Yes, it does. There must be dozens of girls who would gladly go out with you.'

'It was you I asked.'

'I know that. But why?'

Adam was silent for a while, his face shadowed as we moved around the tiny dance floor. 'That,' he said eventually, 'is a very naïve question. You probably suspect me of being sorry for you. I'm not. The truth is that I know just enough about you to want to know more. I remember you when you were a tomboy. I've heard about you—from your grandmother and from Melly. I want to find out for myself. Do you mind?'

'I'm very flattered,' I said quietly, ashamed of my ingracious attitude.

When the tune ended, we strolled towards the brightly-lit bar, where a young man who sat on a stool by the wall was watching us with interest. I had never seen a more handsome man—sleek dark hair, long-lashed dark eyes, even features deeply tanned. He was wearing a grey safari suit with an orange shirt and his stare was too bold to return. I pretended not to have noticed.

But as Adam was ordering drinks and settling me on one of the high stools, a deep voice spoke his name and this same young man stood there smiling. He was even more attractive at close quarters.

'I thought you were a misogynist, Adam. Where have you been hiding this young lady?'

'I'm choosy, that's all,' Adam replied. 'Lyn, may I introduce Guy Breder? This is Lynda Fielding, Guy.'

'I couldn't be more delighted,' said Guy Breder.

And I said, 'How do you do, Mr Breder,' which made him laugh.

'We can't be so formal,' he said. 'We're related, aren't we? Step-cousins, or something?'

I was still recovering from the shock. This was the man for whom Melly had nothing but praise. Now that I saw him, I didn't wonder. He was the kind of man every girl dreams of meeting some day until she decides to settle for something more attainable. The difference was that he was here, real, and looking at me with open admiration.

'Can I buy you a drink?' Adam asked.

Guy glanced at his watch. 'Not now, thanks. I must be going. Anyway, I don't want to butt in. I'll be seeing you, Lynda. 'Bye Adam.'

I watched him make his way to the door, where he turned and raised a hand in farewell, and when I glanced back at Adam I found him studying my face, but he looked away swiftly.

'No wonder Melly's so pleased with her new step-brother,' I remarked. 'He's very attractive, isn't he?'

'You're a better judge of that than I am,' Adam replied.

'What's his job?'

'No idea. Spending his father's money, from what I gather... No, that's not fair. He has various business interests inherited from his father, and he's often away on business. I've never bothered to find out exactly what business it is.'

'The blonde and curvy kind, probably,' I said drily.

Adam turned his glass round and round on the bar top. 'Could be, but he spends the rest of his time at the Mount and takes no interest in the local girls. You'd expect a man like that to rope in all the females he could—it wouldn't be difficult for him, would it? And he wouldn't need to go off on illicit weekends.'

'No, I suppose not. So what do we conclude? He's dedicated to his career and has no time for women.' I lifted my glass and smiled at him over the rim. 'Come to think of it, Adam, you and Guy have a lot in common.'

★ ★ ★ ★

We didn't stay out late. It was around ten o'clock when the car drew up at the cottage gate and Adam came round to open the door for me.

'Will you come in for some coffee?' I asked.

'I think not. You ought to get to bed, and so did I since I'm on call tomorrow night. When can I see you again?'

'My engagement book isn't exactly overflowing,' I replied.

'Saturday, then? Do you fancy seeing a performance of "The Student Prince"? Local Amateur Operatics.'

'It sounds like fun,' I said. 'Thank you, I'd like to, if you're sure my state of health can stand it.'

Despite the darkness, I saw Adam's grin as he replied, 'Well, if you feel like fainting again you'll be in the right company, though next time I'll charge you a fee.'

I was laughing with him when suddenly he took hold of me and kissed me very firmly on the mouth, said, 'Good night, Lyn,' and went back to the car. When the red tail-lights disappeared down the road I was still standing where he had left me, surprised into immobility by the unexpectedness of that kiss. I had expected Adam to be a slow-moving kind of man. In fact, I had still suspected that he was merely being kind by taking me out. But now I began to wonder...

When I walked into the cottage, Smokey came barking round my ankles and I picked him up, cuddling him.

'Had a nice time, then?' Gran asked, emerging from the kitchen.

'Very nice, thank you. And we met Uncle James' step-son. He's very good-looking, isn't he?'

Gran grunted. 'I wouldn't know about that. I only seen him in his car—great roaring monster. And handsome is as handsome does. Dr Taylor may not be no film star, but he's a nice man, isn't he?'

'Thoroughly nice,' I agreed.

* * * *

I was trying to cut down on my sleeping tablets, though I was terrified of insomnia. A sleepless night always left me with a foul headache. But that night I decided to do without pills, having had two sherries and a vodka with orange. But the very fear of not sleeping kept me awake. My mind was alive with images of the day. I thought about Uncle Jonathon's family documents, which might be used as the base for a historical novel, and his strange reference to a hotel, which I ought to have asked about but hadn't. And then there was Adam. Would it be wise to encourage him? And Guy, whose handsome face and flashing dark eyes seemed to be engraved on my retina...

After tossing and turning for what seemed like hours, I grabbed the sleeping tablet bottle and swallowed two pills. Relieved, I fell asleep—long before the drug could take effect.

I know now how stupid I was, but that combination of the state of my nerves and the twists of fate led me into a coma-deep sleep on the very night when I was needed. For when I woke up to a rainy morning, my head muzzy from the after-effects of the pills, and stumbled downstairs in my dressing-gown for a reviving cup of coffee, I found the cottage freezing cold. There was no fire in the grate, no Smokey to greet me as he always did, no sound other than the downpour.

I dragged myself into the tiny kitchen, calling to Gran. The light was on, the back door wide open. The drumming of rain on the plant-filled conservatory drowned my croaky voice. Making for the door, I stood clinging to the jamb, staring in disbelief at the earthenware tiled floor. My grandmother lay there, rain blowing in on her from the open door, soaking her nightdress and dressing-gown.

And even in that first glance I knew that she was dead.

CHAPTER THREE

They tell me that I was "very brave" that morning. It isn't true. I was simply numbed by shock. I only remember snatches of incidents. The baker's face, turning ghastly white at the sight of me as I asked him to send for a doctor. He must have gone to phone from the Mount, for shortly afterwards Melly arrived, with Martin. She was helping me to dress, chattering on in an effort to comfort me, and I clearly remember shouting at her to, 'Shut up, for God's sake!'

The doctor arrived—Dr Frank Taylor,

Adam's father, who was semi-retired but had come because he was nearest. And then the local constable and other men, who tramped back and forth and asked questions. Of course, I could tell them nothing. I had no idea why Gran had been in the conservatory. The last time I saw her she was going to bed and I hadn't heard her get up. Now she was being carried away, on a stretcher.

Martin's arm supported me as he led me out to his Land-Rover, with Melly fussing round us. I found myself at the Mount, being led up the stairs by my cousins to a room which Mrs Porter had hastily prepared.

And there I sat, alone, staring out of the window to the sea which crashed beyond the cliff. Someone brought me a lunch tray, but I left it untouched. My mind was empty, concentrating on trivial things like the line of flight of a seagull. Didn't birds mind the rain?

I have no idea what time it was when Adam came. I simply looked round and he was there.

'How are you feeling, Lyn?'

'Fine, thank you.'

'I did knock, but...'

'I'm sorry. I didn't hear you.' I sounded calm, too calm.

He glanced at the lunch tray on the side table. 'You haven't eaten anything. You ought to.'

'I'm not hungry. But I'm all right. Everyone has been very kind.'

Adam came closer to me, bent and laid his hands on my shoulders. 'Lyn,' he said urgently. 'Let go. For heaven's sake, scream and shout if you want to. You'll break in two if you carry on like this.'

'I'm perfectly all right,' I said in the same flat voice I had used all day. 'I've done enough breaking down lately. I must be strong about this.'

He took a paper from his pocket and laid it on the window-seat beside me. 'You'd better sign this.'

'What is it?'

'Application for a change of doctor. One of my partners will take you on. Dr Frazer. All you have to do is sign it. What was the name of your former doctor?'

I told him, and the address, and signed the document because he wanted me to.

'Don't you want to know what happened to your grandmother?' he asked worriedly.

'She died.'

'Lyn, please! She had a heart attack. It was very quick and she didn't suffer.'

'I'm glad,' I said quietly.

'There's more to it, but you're in no state now to hear it. Will you take some tranquillisers and go to bed? A good sleep...'

'Sleep!' I exclaimed, coming out of my lethargy. 'It was because I was so damned sound asleep that this happened. I might have heard. I might have helped her.'

'You couldn't have done,' Adam said gently. 'Nobody could. You mustn't blame yourself, Lyn. She was an old lady. And there's nothing for you to worry about. My father is one of the executors. He'll take care of...'

'Smokey!' I said. 'Where's Smokey? Did they find him?'

'I don't know. I'll find out, shall I, and have him brought to you? Would you like that?'

The thought of the poor little dog was more than I could bear. The floodgates opened at last and I was able to cry. Adam simply sat and held me, saying nothing but stroking my hair and letting me weep.

★ ★ ★ ★

There followed a strange few days of unreality. I remained at the Mount, where I was treated with the utmost kindness. My brother Bob flew in for the funeral, blond and bronzed, but he had to go back almost immediately and his leaving left me totally alone.

No-one found Smokey. He seemed to have run away. I might have followed his example if I had had anywhere to run to.

But gradually I came back to normal. My sadness remained, but I had been through bereavement before and knew that to stay in the doldrums was merely self-indulgent.

* * * *

One morning as I went down one branch of the staircase I heard Lottie's voice calling impatiently, 'James! James!'

My Uncle James emerged ponderously from one of the passageways into the hall and said testily, 'What is it, my dear? I was about to...'

'This is more important,' Lottie replied. She came into view at the foot of the stairs, elegant as always in a wine-coloured slacks suit, and I found myself pausing, unintentionally eavesdropping.

'I have just called the builders,' she continued in a furious voice, 'to ask why they are so long in coming to make the estimates. And they tell me the arrangement has been cancelled by my husband.'

'Cancelled?' Uncle James echoed. 'Nonsense, Lottie. There must have been some mistake. I'm as eager to get started as you are.'

'They seemed very sure,' Lottie said dubiously. 'So we have been waiting for six weeks for builders who had no intention of coming.'

'Did you tell them it was a mistake?'

'Most definitely I did. They have promised to come in a day or two, as soon as they can, and I told them if there was any delay we should take our business elsewhere.'

'Then that's all that needs doing,' Uncle James said.

'But who cancelled it?' Lottie wanted to know.

Uncle James made an impatient sound in his throat. 'Nobody. You know how unreliable these people are. It was probably just an excuse. Now really...I am extremely busy.'

They departed and I made my way to the small landing at the top of the main stairs, wondering what Lottie was planning to do to the Mount now. The central heating was a great success, except here in the hall, which was too vast for radiators to make any impression. Portraits hung on the panelled walls and the floor was made of mosaic, with a round picture depicting a ship tossing on a wild sea with cliffs in the background.

From the terrace there was a stretch of gorse and heather curving down to the lip of the cliff. I made my way between the bushes and went gingerly over the edge, onto the steeply-slanting path which led down to the rocky cove. It was a private place, with headlands rearing either side of it and gulls like swirling snow wheeling in the air to the accompaniment of the crash and roar of the breakers and the undertow which ground the stones one against another.

Many a boat-load of contraband had been landed here. Martin used to tell bloodthirsty tales of battles with the revenuers, and there was a legend of a tunnel leading from the cove to the Mount, though no one had ever found it. At the back of the cove, almost hidden by the thick growth of hardy bushes, there was a crack in the cliff which probably gave rise to the legend. As children, we had ventured daringly into the deep, dark cave behind the crevice, but it was too black and eerie to stay long inside.

As I made my way slowly down the cliff I heard the gulls set up a clamour of alarm. A cloud of them rose from their perches on the smooth rocks, making me pause to wonder what was bothering them. I saw two of them swoop low over the grey form of a cat which was prowling among the boulders. It was a thin, unkempt animal, almost the same colour as the stones, and as I watched it lifted a taloned paw to swipe at a gull that came too close. The bird stuttered in the air and fell heavily, whereupon a crowd of its fellows closed in about the cat, which gave up the uneven fight and darted for the shelter of the bushes.

I was wondering where the cat had come from when I heard a voice calling my name and looked up to see Guy outlined against the cloud-streaked sky.

'I was just going for a ride,' he said as he scrambled down towards me, steadying himself with one hand on the cliff-face. 'Will you come with me? You do ride, don't you?'

'I used to, but it's ages since...'

His smile warmed me, cajoled me irresistibly as he held out his hand. 'Come and try. We needn't go far. It will do you good.'

* * * *

I was pleased to find that I had not forgotten how to ride. Soon we were galloping along the top of the combe, following the coast-line, and the breeze in my hair was exhilarating. Tomorrow, I thought ruefully, I would probably be stiff and sore, but it was worth it for the joy of being out in the Spring sunshine. With Guy as a companion.

Eventually we dismounted and walked the horses down into a valley where trees crowded round a clear-flowing stream. Throwing the reins over a thick bush, we sat down on a large flat boulder and contemplated the view of the valley and the hills. The trees were on the point of bursting into leaf and the birds sang joyfully.

'I'm glad you're feeling better,' Guy said, looking into my face. 'I was quite worried about you.'

'Oh, I'm fine now.' I laughed nervously, stroking my tumbled hair back into place.

'You needn't do that,' Guy said. 'I find that scar just as attractive as the rest of you. It gives you an air of mystery... You're blossoming, Lyn. And the wind has made your eyes shine... Or is it more than the wind?'

Looking into those dark, lustrous eyes of his, I could find no answer. His arms slid round me and his lips met mine warmly.

'I knew how it would be,' he said. 'The first time I laid eyes on you, dancing with Adam Taylor, I knew this would happen. You knew it, too, didn't you? You tried to hide it, but I saw the look in your eyes. Lovely eyes. Lovely Lyn.'

'You're rushing me,' I replied levelly. But it was balm to my injured soul and I didn't try to stop him when he kissed me again.

⋆ ⋆ ⋆ ⋆

Leaving Guy talking to Martin in the stable-yard, I made my way across the cobbles and into the kitchen, where Melly and Mrs Porter were preparing lunch. The room was full of delicious smells and made me exclaim that I was starving.

'Why Miss Lynda,' said Mrs Porter with a smile. ' 'Tis grand to hear you say that.'

'It must be all the fresh air,' Melly said, keeping her back turned. 'You've been long enough.'

'Only an hour,' I said. 'We got as far as Cragdale Cleave. You ought to have come with us.'

Melly swung round, her spotty face sullen. She had been eating biscuits or something, for there were crumbs all down her jumper.

'I was too busy,' she said tartly. 'And anyway, I can't ride properly. Excuse me.'

She brushed past me and went out, leaving me to glance questioningly at Mrs Porter.

'Oh, don't take no notice of Miss Melly,' she said. 'Her's been in a bad mood all morning. You run along and get changed, Miss Lynda.'

In the cold spaces of the hall, Melly was waiting for me.

'I forgot to tell you,' she said in the same unfriendly tone. 'There was a phone call for you—from your *other* boyfriend. He wanted to see you tonight, but I told him you were out with Guy and I didn't know what your plans were.'

'Do you mean Adam?' I asked. 'Melly, what on earth is wrong with you? Have I done something to upset you?'

But Melly just tossed her head and turned away. I went after her, determined to get to the bottom of this.

'Melly, please tell me. What's the matter?'

She looked at me, eyes brimming. 'Nothing's the matter! I just wish you'd never come.'

Whirling away from me, she ran up the stairs just as Lottie appeared in the archway which led to the North wing.

'There's a phone call for you,' she said coldly. 'You can take it in the sitting-room. I've switched it through. We must really have another line brought to the house. I need the phone for business purposes.'

Sunlight shafted into the sitting-room through the four tall windows as I hurried to pick up the phone.

'Is that you, Lyn?' said Adam's voice. 'Well, I'm glad to have caught you at last. What are you doing this evening?'

'Nothing special. Melly said you phoned earlier. Is it something important?'

There was a small silence before Adam replied. 'Do I have to have a special reason to see you?'

'No, of course not. But with you ringing again so soon...I just wondered... What had you planned?'

'Well...I'm taking evening surgery, so I may not get away much before seven-thirty. How about us going for a drink? I'll pick you up about half-past eight.'

'That's fine,' I said. 'I look forward to seeing you, Adam.'

'It's mutual,' Adam replied.

* * * *

At lunchtime, Uncle Jonathon came in with his left hand heavily bandaged.

'Jammed a chisel into it,' he explained ruefully, but brushed aside all our anxious enquiries. 'No, of course I don't need a doctor. The foreman fixed me up from the first-aid box... Oh, no, not very hungry.

Just a small helping, please.'

Uncle James, Lottie and Martin went back to their respective jobs and Guy announced his intention of driving to Exeter to buy new tyres for his car.

'Would you like to come with me, Lyn?' he asked. 'We could have dinner somewhere on the way back.'

I was about to tell him that I already had an engagement for that evening when Uncle Jonathon, who hadn't been looking at Guy, and therefore hadn't seen what he said, spoke up.

'I thought we might have a look at those papers this afternoon, Lynda? Do you feel up to it?'

'I'd love to,' I said. 'Sorry, Guy, but I'd rather stay in.'

I saw Melly's face then. She was staring hopefully at Guy with the air of a dog anxious to be taken for a walk.

'Why don't you take Melly?' I suggested.

She went bright red and glared mutinously at me. 'I couldn't. I've got to help Mrs Porter.'

'Then I shall have to go alone,' Guy said, pushing his chair back. 'See you later.'

Melly sat quite still, her mouth working

as though she were trying to voice words to take back her blunt refusal. But when the door closed behind Guy she looked furiously at me and muttered, 'Why don't you mind your own business? Nobody asked you to interfere. Now you've made me look a fool.'

'What did she say?' Uncle Jonathon asked. 'I didn't follow that conversation.'

I looked at him and said clearly, 'It didn't make much sense to me, either... Where do you keep your papers?'

His brown, gnarled face broke into a grin. 'In the gun room. Shall we go?'

The gun room housed the family collection of weapons. It was reached by a long, tortuous corridor, up a few steps, round a corner, along a passageway with window-seats cut into the thick walls. It was the oldest part of the house, built in the days when defence was necessary.

There were two suits of armour, swords and shields, pistols of varying design, and in pride of place on a table lay a shining wooden box which Uncle Jonathon opened reverently. Nestling in red velvet were a matched pair of pistols, long-barrelled, with butts of intricately-carved ivory.

'These guns,' my uncle told me in his

soft voice, 'were nearly the end of the Hathersages. Have you heard the story?'

I shook my head. 'I don't think so.'

'At the time,' he said, 'there were three sons. The oldest was drowned at sea. The other two were twins—Mark and Michael. They were both in love with the same girl and decided to settle it by fighting a duel out on the clifftop, with these very pistols. Michael was killed. Mark tried to run away, but he was brought back and hung for his brother's murder.'

'How awful!' I said. 'So what happened?'

Uncle Jonathon chuckled. 'The girl—the one they had the fight about—gave birth to a son a few months later. She brought him to the Mount and said he was the child of one of the twins. She didn't know which. Anyway, the old man believed her and raised the boy as his heir. That was Roland, my great-great-grandfather.' He looked up at me, hazel eyes bright with laughter. 'There's a bit of everything in our family. Take André now—the father of the twins. His mother was a French emigrée at the time of the Revolution. He was a regular rake till he married the Potterton heiress. He was forty then, but still managed to father three sons.'

He closed the gun-case and placed it lovingly back on the table, moving across to a small chest with shallow drawers. 'Ah, there's such a lot I could tell you. The first James, for instance—he fought for Monmouth in the rebellion and got himself killed, so his young wife ups and marries a Captain Brooks, who was known to be a highwayman. He changed his name to Hathersage. So by rights we all ought to be called Brooks, I suppose.'

I touched his arm to make him look at me. 'Is all this in the documents?'

'Oh, no. But you've only got to read between the lines. I've heard the tales from my father and grandfather. In this chest there are letters, diaries, copies from various registers, and notes I've made from reference books. But there's one thing I want you to see first—a letter from one of the customs men to his chief... Ah here it is.'

I read the letter with difficulty. The writing was bad, the spelling weird and the ink faded, but it seemed to be a complaint that no contraband had been found at the Mount, though the officer was certain it must be there since his men had watched the smugglers unload their booty in the cove. They had lain in wait at the clifftop, but the smugglers and their goods had disappeared into thin air. The customs men had searched the cove and the house, with the willing co-operation of Roland Hathersage, but had found nothing. There was a suggestion that witchcraft might have been employed. The writer of the letter was obviously anxious that none of the blame for failure be laid at his door.

'So you see,' Uncle Jonathon said. 'There must be a tunnel.'

'Then why didn't they find it?' I asked.

'What?' said my uncle, who hadn't caught my words.

Looking into his face, I repeated my question, adding, 'Anyway, after all this time it's probably collapsed.'

He frowned and shook his head. 'You sound like your Uncle James. He'd only be interested if there was money to be made out of it. But I'm sure it's there. I've searched the house for the exit from it, but I can't find it.'

'Haven't you looked in the cove? There is a deep crack in the cliff.'

'Yes, I know there is, but I can't go down there. You remember how Jenny was always terrified of playing on the cliff? I've got that, too. Fear of heights. It makes me dizzy just to think about the cliff path. So I need someone to go and look for me. Will you do it, Lyn?'

'Now?' I said.

'Oh no, no. There's no hurry. But some time when you're out for a walk... It looks like rain now. Let's settle down and go through these notes, shall we?'

* * * *

I had never considered myself to be particularly psychic, but I had always experienced a strange sense of awe when I was in the oldest wing of the Mount. Places like the gun room, Aunt Maude's suite, and the bedroom I was using seemed to hold an aura of other-worldliness which is impossible to explain. Once when I was a child I had strayed near the gun room during a game of hide and seek and seen in the corridor a ragged boy who had no business being at the Mount. I had followed him round a corner, only to find that he had disappeared. I remember my indignation at the temerity of that urchin, though when I told Uncle James and Aunt Nora about it they had scolded me for a liar. Later I realised that it must have been a ghost I saw and that my elders had probably not wanted to start a scare by admitting they had heard of such phenomena.

I repeated the story to Uncle Jonathon now and he told me quite calmly that, yes, there was a child ghost, thought to be a servant boy who had been beaten so badly that he died, but there was no documentary evidence of it.

As we sat there exploring the past, reading letters and notebooks of people long dead, I had the creepy feeling that all our ancestors were there watching us, part of the tissue of the house, and it was almost a relief when the gong summoned us to dinner.

'Shall we go on this evening?' Uncle Jonathon asked eagerly.

'No, I'm sorry, I can't. I'm going out with Adam.'

'Adam?' he said, in a tone which might also have been consternation. Then he nodded and patted my arm, saying, 'I'm glad. He's a nice boy. Be good to him, Lynda.'

* * * *

Adam was later than he had said he would be, so I ran out as soon as I saw his car arrive in the yard.

'You look much chirpier,' he said as I settled beside him. 'Had a good day?'

'Yes, thank you. Have you?'

'Much as usual. I'm sorry I'm late. I had to call in at the hospital on my way home.'

He sounded tired, almost grim.

'If you'd rather we didn't go...' I began.

'No!' he said quickly, glancing at me. 'I want to go. As a matter of fact, Lyn, I've got some things to tell you. Oh, I didn't know about it when I rang you. I heard over dinner. I was hoping to have a nice quiet evening with you, but...'

'It sounds terrible,' I said worriedly. 'Whatever is it, Adam?'

But he wouldn't tell me until we had reached our destination, a small pub in a village out on the moors. It was an ancient building, thick stone walls, low-beamed ceilings, and a fireplace big enough to roast an ox, though there was only a log fire burning there now. The bar was hung with horse-brasses, the rooms lit by oil lamps fitted for electricity, and the people spoke with the Devonshire burr in their voices and regarded us with veiled hostility.

We sat down in the inglenook beside the fire, our drinks on a tiny round table, while Adam regarded me long and levelly, his angular face expressing a seriousness which was alarming.

'You do look a lot better,' he said eventually. 'I'm glad to see that. Do you think you can stand another shock?'

'I've been preparing myself for it ever since we set out,' I said. 'I shall feel better when I know what it is.'

'It's about your grandmother,' he said, and his freckled hand came out to cover mine. 'Lyn...I don't quite know how to say this, but...she must have been in the garden when she died. There was mud all down her clothes.'

'Then how did she get into the conservatory? You told me it was quick.'

'It was. I promise you, Lyn. Someone carried her into the conservatory, probably thinking she was still alive. There was a muddy bootprint on the floor.'

'But why did they just leave her? Why didn't they wake me?'

'They probably didn't know you were

there. The police have been making enquiries but getting nowhere. Whoever it was, he doesn't want it known that he was there. And there's something else you ought to know. Smokey was found today.'

The news ought to have cheered me, but Adam spoke so gravely that I knew he was giving me bad news. I waited to hear it.

'The verger, Mr Tregannon, found him. He was scything the weeds in the corner of the churchyard near the cottage and came across Smokey's body. The poor little devil's neck was broken.'

CHAPTER FOUR

I sat staring disbelievingly at Adam, the fire warming me on one side, my other side cold as ice, and my hand gripping the strong fingers of my companion.

'Smokey was killed?' I breathed. 'A tiny little dog?'

'He may have been thrown over the railing, but why, and by whom... The police have been over every inch of ground and there's nothing to go by. But of course it poured with rain and it was several hours before the alarm was raised.'

'Yes,' I said dully. 'Because I was so sound asleep. Oh, Adam...'

He gazed at me sorrowfully. 'I'm sorry I had to be the one to tell you, Lyn, but I thought it was better than you hearing it from a stranger. It's all over the village about your Gran's dog being found and people will start wild rumours if I know anything. At least you know the facts now.'

'Yes. And thank you, Adam.'

'You've taken it very calmly,' he said, putting his other hand out so that mine was imprisoned between his. 'You're sure you feel all right?'

'Can't you forget you're a doctor, just for a few minutes?'

'My concern is personal, not professional. I've been worried about you this last week. Every time I've seen you, you've seemed to be in a world of your own.'

'I know. It's all a bit vague in my mind. But I have shaken it off now, so you needn't worry any more.'

He released my hand and picked up his glass. 'I hear you went riding this morning?'

'Yes, I did. It was a lovely morning. Sunshine, and Spring really on the way at last. Mind you, I feel a bit stiff now.'

Adam was staring into the fire, flickering light playing over the planes and hollows of his face and bringing out the redness in his thick hair. 'How are you getting on with the family?'

'About the same as usual. Uncle James always was a bit pompous and Lottie seems preoccupied with work. This morning they were talking about having builders in. Are they planning alterations?'

'I've no idea,' Adam said with a shrug. 'What about the others?'

'Oh, Uncle Jonathon is as sweet as ever. We spent the afternoon going through his collection of papers, and he's asked me to do a thorough search of the cave—looking for the famous tunnel.'

'There's been talk about that for years. I think you'll have a vain search. But I thought...' He broke off, looked away from me. 'Jonathon has always guarded those papers jealously, saving them for Jenny. Has he decided she's never coming back?'

Jenny again. The question was back in my mind. Had there ever been anything between Adam and Jenny?

'He isn't giving them to me,' I said, 'just letting me look at them. He did say that Jenny was never really interested in history.'

'No, she wasn't,' Adam said, his eyes on his half-finished beer. 'She was afraid of stagnating in Hathercombe. She wanted to travel. That's why she leapt at the chance of this job in America.'

'Does she write to you?' I asked.

He looked round in surprise. 'To me? No. Why should she?'

Adam was a very bad dissembler. His voice, when he had talked about Jenny, had been tinged with bitterness. I was sure that he had known her very well and that she had hurt him in some way. Was that why Uncle Jonathon had told me to be kind to Adam?

'I just thought she might,' I said. 'After all, you've known each other all your lives.'

'Jenny isn't much of a letter writer,' Adam replied. 'Jonathon gets a postcard occasionally, but that's all. However, we were talking about the people at the Mount.'

'So we were, but I don't know what

you want me to say. I'm more or less accepted there, treated like one of the family...except...Melly was in a funny mood today. You'd have thought she hated me, and you know how friendly she usually is.'

'Was this before or after you went riding with Guy?'

'Why, it...Adam, what could that... Oh, really! You're not trying to tell me she's jealous, are you? Guy's her step-brother.'

'Which means nothing,' Adam said levelly, his eyes holding mine. 'He's an attractive man—you said so yourself. And Melly is a frustrated female. She's never had a boy-friend. And suddenly this devastating character is actually in the same house. He's good-looking, rich, charming. Isn't that what every female dreams about? Why should you imagine Melly's dreams are any different from yours?' By the time he finished speaking, his voice was ragged with emotion and he turned abruptly away from me.

'I hadn't looked at it that way,' I said quietly. 'I didn't mean to hurt Melly. If I had realised... I suppose I ought to have guessed from the look on her face when he asked me to go into Exeter with him today. She was dying to be asked, but...'

'Why didn't you go?' he demanded.

'He wasn't coming back until late, and I had already arranged to come out with you. Anyway, I was more interested in Uncle Jonathon's papers.'

He was silent for a long time. We finished our drinks and Adam went to get some more. When he came back, he sat down further away from me than he had been before.

'I'm sorry I made you angry,' I said. 'I wouldn't hurt Melly for anything. But I don't know what I can do about it.'

'You could always discourage Guy,' Adam said roughly. 'But why should you? Melly hasn't a hope in hell and she might as well be convinced of that.'

The conversation turned then from the personal to the general and it wasn't long before the barman called 'Time'. We drove back across the dark moors, not saying much. I was wondering why Adam had been so angry. Was it possible that he was more fond of Melly than he cared to admit? It hardly seemed likely, but I could think of no other reason for his annoyance.

When we reached the Mount, Adam parked the car at the side of the house and walked with me to the front door. 'Lyn...' he said slowly. 'I shan't be asking you out any more.'

I stared up at him, surprised and hurt. I had come to value Adam's friendship more than I realised.

'Why ever not?'

'Isn't it obvious? I could easily get too fond of you, and that would be asking for trouble. I can't begin to compete with Guy Breder, so I won't even try.'

'I wasn't aware there was any competition,' I said in a small voice. 'I like Guy, but I also like you. Don't ask me to decide anything so soon.'

'I'm not,' he said. 'I'm withdrawing from the race. Goodbye, Lyn.'

He began to walk away, but stopped when I spoke, his straight back turned to me.

'I was wrong,' I said quietly. 'You and Guy are completely different. He has too much self-confidence and you have none.' I moved towards him, laid my hand lightly on his sleeve. 'What did Jenny do to you, Adam?'

In the hazy moonlight his face was livid as he swung round. 'Who told you about that?'

'No one did. But there have been odd remarks from different people and then tonight, when we talked about her... It *was* Jenny, wasn't it? She hurt you badly.'

'That was five years ago,' he said in a strangled voice. 'I forgot about Jenny long ago.'

'Did you? Then why punish me for what she did? I don't know what it was, but...'

'She made me aware of my limitations,' he said grimly. 'That's all. And I don't intend to discuss it. Goodbye, Lyn.'

'I'll miss you,' I said quietly as he strode away, but he didn't appear to have heard.

The following morning, Uncle Jonathon's hand and arm had swollen up alarmingly. The skin around the deep cut on his palm had taken on a sickly bluish tinge and there was pus oozing from the cut itself. Despite all his protests, the family combined against him and he was put into Martin's Land-Rover, to be driven to the Casualty Department at Ilfracombe hospital.

Melly and I were in the kitchen when an old man appeared at the back door, carrying a large cardboard box. He was introduced as Mr Tregannon, the verger, and I had already guessed what he was bringing—the body of a Cairn terrier, found dead among the weeds in the churchyard.

'I'll take him to the cottage,' I said to Melly, 'and bury him in the garden.'

She was still displeased with me, but her natural kindness could never remain buried for long. 'Do you want me to come?'

'No. It's kind of you, Melly, but I can manage, thank you. See you later.'

⋆ ⋆ ⋆ ⋆

Taking a spade from Gran's shed, I laboriously dug a hole beneath the budding apple trees, watched from the branches by a bright-eyed blackbird. I put the box carefully at the bottom of the hole and as I began to pile earth on top a movement in the bushes beyond the fence caught my eye. It was the skinny grey cat again, coming sinuously through the underbrush of the wilderness, its eyes fixed on the blackbird above me. At the fence, it paused and fixed me with malevolent yellow eyes, close enough for me to see its patchy coat and torn ears. The poor thing must be living wild, I thought.

The blackbird set up a loud chatter of warning and launched itself from the apple tree towards the yews in the churchyard. The cat remained where it was, watching me as I completed my task and trod the earth into a small mound.

I held out my hand, saying, 'Puss, puss,' but the only response was an angry lashing of the long grey tail, so I went back inside the cottage and poured the remains of a bottle of milk into an old cereal dish. When I again returned to the garden, the cat was sniffing round Smokey's grave.

'Here, puss!' I called softly. The cat tensed and looked over its shoulder as I put the dish on the ground. I waited, but it wouldn't come near me, so I left the dish where it was.

The cottage was mine now, or it would be when Gran's will was proved. She had left everything to me, which had seemed a bit unfair, but my brother Bob had said cheerfully that he didn't need a cottage, though he hoped he would be welcome to stay with me any time he chose.

I wandered round the cottage, surveying my legacy. Since I also had been left a substantial sum when my parents died I could live comfortably enough for a while without bothering about a job. Perhaps I could really get down to writing that novel, but there was one thing I decided definitely that morning—I would come back to live at Smugglers' Cottage. It was where I belonged.

As I stood in the small bedroom which still contained relics of my childhood. I heard someone call my name. Guy was standing at the foot of the stairs, watching me as I bent my head to avoid the low beam.

'Melly told me you were here,' he said. 'You shouldn't have come alone.'

'It doesn't worry me,' I replied. 'There are a lot of happy memories here. I always loved this cottage.'

'You used to come here when you were little, didn't you?' he asked, his fingers tracing the side of my cheek. 'I wish I had known you then. What were you like?'

'A revolting little tomboy. You wouldn't have looked twice.' Especially, my mind added, with cousin Jenny around. And then I was annoyed with myself. I seemed to be developing an obsession about Jenny.

'I wasn't a very pleasant child myself,'

Guy said with a smile. 'Perhaps it's as well we didn't meet until now.'

He bent to kiss me, but, without knowing why, I turned my face away. 'Please, Guy. Don't.'

'I'm sorry,' he said softly, misunderstanding. 'It was thoughtless of me. I respect your grandmother's memory, even though I never met her. Are you coming back to the Mount now?'

'Yes, I suppose so.'

As we left the cottage by way of the conservatory, I paused to wonder who had been here that night. Who had silenced Smokey and shocked my grandmother to her death? And why?

The garden was quiet and unmysterious, daffodils blooming under the apple trees where leaves were beginning to show like star clusters on the bare branches. I noticed that the dish I had left out was empty. Everything was very normal. The innocent face of early Spring seemed to hide no dark secrets.

'I've been thinking,' Guy said as we walked up to the Mount. 'Perhaps we ought to be a bit discreet for a while. People might think we're callous to be happy so soon after...'

'You're taking an awful lot for granted,' I said quietly.

He stopped walking and turned to look at me, his hand suddenly tight around mine. 'It doesn't have to be spoken to be true. We both know what has happened. The first time we met...'

'I find you attractive, physically. That's all.'

'But yesterday...'

'Yesterday you kissed me. That proves nothing.'

Guy stood there, staring at me as if he didn't believe his senses. 'Look, love,' he said anxiously, 'I'm sorry. But I honestly thought things were agreed between us. If you're not sure yet, I'll wait. We can go on being friends, can't we?'

'I hope so,' I said.

'Then please...' Very slowly, he took my face between his hands...

At that moment, Martin's Land-Rover rattled up the drive and came past us with a sharp blare from the horn. He must have gone straight into the Mount and told them what he had seen, for Melly treated me with renewed coldness for the rest of the day.

Martin also brought worrying news about

Uncle Jonathon. The cut in his hand had gone bad and was poisoning his bloodstream, so he would have to stay in hospital for a few days.

* * * *

I spent the afternoon among the ghosts in the gun room, working with Uncle Jonathon's notes and writing down a few ideas of my own. Taking a break from this task, I discovered two strangers in the hall, measuring up and taking notes—presumably the builders come to make an estimate. It wasn't my place to ask them what they were doing, but I ran into Lottie in the corridor and asked her.

'We are making a few alterations,' she said. 'Oh...I suppose it will do no harm to tell you why. Soon the whole village will know... We are turning the Mount into a hotel. It is ridiculous to have so many rooms unused when we could turn them into a lucrative business, don't you agree? Of course, there has never been enough money to embark on such a venture, but now...' She spread her hands expressively.

'Oh,' I said blankly. 'I see. But doesn't anybody mind? I mean, Uncle Jonathon...'

'He was not too keen at first,' Lottie admitted, 'but it is not really his affair. The Mount belongs to my husband. Jonathon has seen the wisdom of the idea, I assure you.'

'And Martin?' I asked.

Lottie shrugged. 'Martin's stables will be an added attraction. He is content with his horses. And he would not want to inherit a house that was falling down for lack of funds.'

The conversation left me feeling angry. Turning the Mount into a hotel...it might make good sense economically, but it would ruin the atmosphere of the place. I wondered if Lottie had any real feelings about anything other than money.

* * * *

At dinner I announced my intention of returning to the cottage to live. Uncle James made polite protestations about my being welcome to stay, but he didn't press me. Neither did anyone else. None of them really cared, except perhaps Melly, who couldn't conceal her relief.

* * * *

I had packed my belongings and was preparing to go to bed when there came a faint shriek from the end of the wing and the sound of fists hammering on the door. I looked out into the dark corridor, realising that the sounds emanated from great-aunt Maude's suite. My room was nearest to it and there was no sign of anyone else, so I felt my way along the wall for the nearest light switch and lit the passageway into its usual dull yellow glow—40 watt bulbs for economy. As soon as the lights went on, the noise stopped.

More ghosts? I wondered. But I was more concerned for Aunt Maude. My bare feet made no sound on the thin carpet as I went swiftly to the locked door and turned the key.

The sitting-room was dark, but I could see through to the bedroom, where the frail old lady was trying to lift a chair onto a table—barricading the door of the huge wardrobe.

'Aunt Maude!' I said, not too loudly, and she whirled round, white hair standing on end, the flannel nightdress flapping round her feet.

'Thank goodness!' she exclaimed. 'Come

and help me. He mustn't be allowed to get in. If my father comes and finds him there'll be murder done.' This melodramatic speech explained why she had not pressed her bell for help. She was back in the time before the bell had been installed.

'Aunt Maude,' I said gently. 'Nobody can come in through the wardrobe.'

'Of course he can. Stupid girl! Who are you? What's your name?'

'Lynda. Lynda Field...'

'Ah, yes. The new maid. All right, girl. Can you keep a secret?'

She still looked like a fragile doll, but her voice and manner were those of an imperious young woman used to being obeyed. I decided to humour her. It seemed the best way of settling this disturbance and getting her back into bed, for it was late and the fire had gone out, leaving the room growing colder by the minute.

'Yes,' I assured her. 'But you ought to get back into bed.'

'Listen to me, girl. My young man is trying to get in to see me. He's been forbidden, but he knows the secret stairway and...oh, impetuous fool! I shall be put in a nunnery! Here, fetch that bedwarmer off the wall. And if he gets in, repulse him.'

'I can't hear anything,' I said.

She tutted irritably. 'Then remove the table and open the door. He may have gone by now.'

Putting down the copper bedwarmer, I shifted the chair and table and opened the great oak door of the wardrobe, feeling a complete fool. If anyone came in now they would think I was mad.

'Can you hear anything?' my great-aunt demanded.

'No. No, there's...' But I did hear something, very faint and far away, as if echoing down an empty well. Pushing aside the few dresses which hung there, I climbed into the wardrobe and laid my ear against the back panel. The echo sounded again, a sighing and groaning which might have been the sea in the cove, but might also have been made by a human voice.

But really...inside a wall!

This was, I remembered, coming out in goose pimples, the oldest part of the house. I backed hastily out of the wardrobe.

'I can't hear a thing,' I lied briskly. 'He must have gone. Now, please, Aunt Maude, get back into bed.'

She went willingly enough, trembling

with the effort she had been making, but as I tucked the blankets round her she grasped my wrist with hard fingers.

'You promised!' she hissed. 'It's a secret. You must never tell. There is a curse on servants who betray the secret.'

'I swear,' I said solemnly, and with one last baleful stare from her brilliant blue eyes, my great-aunt fell asleep.

I sat beside her for a while, making sure that she was sleeping peacefully, and wondering what incident from her past she had been reliving. Had there been an impetuous young man who had tried to sneak into the house, risking the wrath of my great-great-grandfather? It sounded plausible, except for the bit about the secret stairs. But if Aunt Maude had been remembering something from her youth then what was it I had heard?

The wardrobe door was still open. Moving as quietly as I could, I stepped inside it again. It was three feet deep by ten wide, fixed to the wall and filling the space from floor to ceiling. A great dark place, seeming tomblike to my roused imagination. Again I put my ear to the back panel. There was only silence. I leaned closer, pressing my ear against the panel.

And suddenly it moved. I only just saved myself from falling into a deep, dark hole. A musty smell assailed me, a smell of age and disuse, cold stone forever in darkness. And as I stepped back, my heart thumping wildly, I saw the first two wedge-like steps of a tightly-winding stair which disappeared into the blackness beneath.

CHAPTER FIVE

I slept fitfully, troubled by strange dreams, and woke to find the house seething with activity. Voices rang along the corridors, running feet pounded, and as I leapt out of bed Melly burst into my room.

'Lyn! Have you seen Aunt Maude?'

'Not since last night,' I said. 'Why, what...' But Melly had gone as hurriedly as she had come.

When I was dressed, I went down to the hall. The family were still rushing about, searching the house with much slamming of doors and calling for Aunt Maude. As I ran down the stairs, Mrs Porter appeared, looking greatly distressed. 'Oh, Miss Lynda!' she cried. 'I *did* lock the door last night. I know I did. Someone else must have left it open.'

Uncle James, panting from the exertion of the search, emerged from a passageway and stood trying to get his breath, his face a bright scarlet; then Lottie appeared from another direction, and Martin.

'She isn't in the house,' Martin declared. 'Mrs Porter, are you sure...?'

'I'm positive!' The housekeeper was in tears now. 'I've always been careful about locking her in, ever since the poor old lady collapsed on the stairs.'

'Then how,' Lottie asked, 'did the door come to be unlocked this morning? Did someone else visit the old lady after you had left her last night?'

'We...I did,' I said, and an accusing silence fell. I looked round at the faces staring at me. 'She was banging on the door and I went to quieten her. When I left her, she was fast asleep. But I did lock the door.' Or had I? I couldn't really remember. 'At least, I *think* I did. But she was asleep and...'

'Standing here talking about it won't help matters,' Martin said. 'We'd better...'

To my intense relief, he was interrupted by Melly's voice from the top of the stairs, saying, 'It's all right. We've found her.'

'Is she all right?' Martin demanded.

The old lady was, it turned out, none the worse for her adventure. She was a little put out at all the fuss and said that she had merely been going to have a chat with poor Sonja, who was confined to bed awaiting the birth of her child. Aunt Maude was still twenty-five years confused, for Sonja's baby had turned out to be my cousin Jenny.

It was Uncle James who had the last word on the affair. He looked coldly at me and said, 'You can thank your lucky stars that she's all right. It's certainly no thanks to you.'

Feeling like a leper, I quietly took my cases and left the Mount.

* * * *

I spent the day playing housewife—shopping in the village and cleaning out the cottage, and in the evening settled down by the fire to work on my novel. As it grew dark, the loneliness began to affect me. I was conscious of the isolation of the cottage—the dark, empty church on one side, the closed Garden Centre on the other—and I wished that I had Smokey to curl up beside me. But my only company was Gran's old radio, which had a permanent crackle, and my own dismal thoughts. I seemed to have made a mess of everything.

Then someone knocked on the door and I found Guy outside, smiling his attractive smile. I was delighted at the thought of his company—someone to talk to; someone to drive away the gathering shadows.

'Hello,' he said, almost shyly. 'I thought you might be feeling lonely. May I come in?'

'Of course. Come and sit down. Would you like some coffee?'

He would, he said, so I made some and when I returned with the tray, Guy told me that he expected to be away for a few days on business.

'It's a nuisance,' he said, 'but my father left various responsibilities which I have to keep an eye on now and then. But I shall bring you a present. What would you like?'

'Some paint,' I said promptly.

Guy laughed. 'Oh, come on, Lyn.

There's always something a girl needs. Something glamorous and not at all practical. A mink stole. A diamond bracelet. What's your particular wish?'

'I told you—decorating materials—but I intend to buy them for myself, thank you. Your money doesn't impress me. I don't like furs and I'd be terrified to own valuable jewellery. I'd probably lose it, or have it stolen.'

'Then what *do* you want?' he asked.

'Corny things—like health and happiness.'

'And love?' he said softly.

I turned my head to look squarely at him. 'That, too, if and when it happens.'

'You're being very wary,' he said. 'Of men in general or me in particular?'

'It pays a girl to be cautious,' I replied.

Guy gave me one of his brilliant smiles as he adroitly changed the subject.

I forget what we talked about for the next hour or so. We were at ease with each other and at some point his arm came around me quite naturally. That should have been the moment when I called a halt, but I found myself thinking how good it was to have him there, to be no longer alone. After all, he was a very attractive man.

But I blame myself for what followed. It wouldn't have happened if I hadn't encouraged him.

'Do you know,' he said, his face very close to mine, 'you have the eyes of a tigress? Golden brown. I bet they glow in the dark.'

Unable to bear his intense scrutiny, I closed my eyes and as I did so his arm tightened, pulling me against him.

He began to kiss me, expertly, lulling me into a sense of security and a growing euphoria. Richard had taught me that my body was capable of giving and receiving pleasure from physical contact, so it was no unawakened virgin who responded to Guy's caresses. I was roused too easily until I realised it was purely physical and had nothing to do with love. At least with Richard I had thought I was in love.

Guy's hand had strayed to the buttons on my blouse when I took hold of it firmly and said, 'No. Don't.'

He let go of me and moved away, suddenly fierce and angry. 'Why not?'

'Because I don't feel that way about you.'

'It's a bit late to discover that,' he said roughly.

'I'm sorry,' I said inadequately.

'And I suppose that makes everything all right, does it?' His voice was harsh with sarcasm and suddenly I was sick of him, sick of myself.

'I think you'd better leave,' I said quietly.

And he did leave, without another word.

* * * *

For a few days I worked quietly, getting down to some serious writing. Several times I glimpsed the grey cat in the garden and I took to setting out a dish of scraps and some milk every day. The food always disappeared and once the cat ran away from the dishes as I went into the conservatory, so I knew it was accepting my offerings. It was a mangy animal, but its presence made me feel less isolated. I was beginning to enjoy myself.

On my fourth day at the cottage I took the bus into Ilfracombe and obtained some reference books from the library. As I walked back from the bus stop in the village, with a heavy shopping bag containing books and provisions, Martin's Land-Rover drew up beside me and there, in the passenger seat, was Uncle Jonathon.

'Oh, it's good to see you back,' I exclaimed, meaning it. 'How do you feel?'

He held up his left hand, fastened in a sling. 'It was silly of me, wasn't it?'

'He's got to take it easy for a few days,' Martin told me. 'But try making him.'

'You must be good!' I said to Uncle Jonathon. 'No rushing about. May I come up and study those papers again tomorrow? I've got the book started.'

He looked pleased. 'Yes, do come. Have you done anything about what we talked about?'

Guessing that he meant the tunnel, I shook my head. 'Not yet. I'll do that tomorrow, too. And I've got something else to tell you.'

'What's this?' Martin demanded. 'Secrets?'

'None of your business,' I said lightly. 'Unless you've suddenly developed a consuming passion for history.'

Martin groaned. 'Oh, that! Not likely. But you shouldn't encourage him. He's batty enough already.'

Since Uncle Jonathon wasn't looking at him he missed that insult, but I suppose he knew well enough that his family regarded him as an eccentric on the subject of the Mount.

★ ★ ★ ★

It had been an unusually warm day for March and I delayed lighting the fire until after my evening meal, when I discovered that there were not enough sticks, though there were plenty of logs in the shed. There was nothing for it but to find the axe and chop my own sticks.

It was a more difficult task than I had imagined. Instead of splitting co-operatively, the logs grabbed the axe-head and I was reduced to banging the whole thing on the concrete. All I produced were large chunks and tiny chips and I began to appreciate that even a mundane task such as this needed a certain amount of skill.

I was resting my aching back when Adam's voice said from behind me, 'What on earth do you think you're doing?'

'I would have thought that was obvious,' I said breathlessly.

He stripped off his jacket and gave it to me, relieving me of the axe at the same time. 'I'll do it. Stand back.'

With infuriating ease, he got the stubborn

logs to split obligingly into nice square sticks, though it made him sweat.

'How nice to have a man about the house,' I said ironically. 'Why wouldn't they do that for me?'

Adam paused in his work, panting. 'You aren't strong enough. That's why. A matter of physical fact, not proof of inferiority. Is that enough?'

'I only wanted to light one small fire,' I said. 'But I'm very grateful. Those will keep me going for a few days. Can I offer you a cup of coffee?'

'Yes, thank you. And be grateful I worked off my feelings on your logs. I came up here intending to give you a lecture.'

'About what?' I asked in astonishment.

'About your staying here alone. You'd be much better off at the Mount for a while.'

'Oh, nonsense! I stayed there quite long enough. Anyway, I like being on my own... Hadn't you better put your jacket on?'

'I'll make your fire first,' he said, picking up an armful of sticks.

I didn't argue. I enjoy having a man do jobs for me. So I made a pot of coffee and cut a few pieces off the cake I had made that afternoon. When Adam came downstairs after washing his hands in the tiny bathroom, I had a little round table set in front of the fire he had lit and was pouring coffee. He paused at the bottom of the stairs, watching me.

'You really ought not to be alone,' he said eventually, coming slowly to the chair I had set for him.

'I'm not alone. You're here. And I'm glad to see you, if you don't mind my saying so...I don't really belong at the Mount. I had decided to come back here even before all that trouble with Aunt Maude, but after that I felt they were all blaming me...oh, I don't suppose they were. It was my own feelings of guilt that caused it. Anyway, I like being here. I can suit myself. So please let's not argue about it. I feel just fine.'

Adam looked doubtful. 'You do look a lot better. But doesn't the loneliness get on your nerves?'

'It did, for a day or two. But I'm not feeling half so nervy as when I arrived, oddly enough, despite all that's happened... Will you have a piece of cake?'

'Yes, please. It looks good.'

'My own make... Don't look so surprised!

My mother was a very good cook and she taught me when I was quite young. So you see, I'm not living on baked beans and fish fingers, whatever you think.'

'I only found out today,' he said, 'that you had moved back here, I mean. I was in the paper shop and your name cropped up in conversation and I was told you'd changed your order.'

'Yes, that's right. Gran's taste for the tabloids doesn't match mine. I prefer a bit more news and a few less pictures.'

He ate three pieces of cake. We finished the pot of coffee and I went to make some more, while Adam stoked the fire, put the lights on and drew the curtains as if he had been doing it all his life. I decided not to comment on it, since he was still sticking to his word. He had not asked me out. *I* had asked him *in*.

I was about to take the second pot of coffee through to the sitting-room when there came a loud crash from the conservatory. I was so startled I almost dropped the pot.

'Lyn!' Adam appeared in the doorway. 'Are you all right? What...'

He brushed past me and stepped into the conservatory, where a half-brick lay on the floor. One of the glass panes was shattered. Swearing, Adam rushed out into the garden and came back a few moments later looking furious.

'Young hooligans! I saw them running off. But it's too dark to tell who they were.' He looked straight at me, his mouth set stubbornly. '*Now* how do you feel about living here alone?'

CHAPTER SIX

The incident was unpleasant and had caused me a momentary fright, but it wasn't enough to make me leave the cottage and I told Adam so.

'Oh, well...' he sighed. 'Where's your brush and pan?'

'Cupboard under the sink. But there's no need for you to...'

Ignoring me, he set about sweeping up the broken glass, so I left him to it and took the coffee through to the other room. I had only just set the pot on the table when an urgent knocking summoned me to the front door.

It was Guy.

'I'm back,' he announced unnecessarily. 'I wondered if we could talk things over. I was probably a bit hasty, and...' He broke off, looking beyond me, and I saw that Adam had emerged from the kitchen, still carrying the dustpan and brush.

'We've just had a bit of bother with some stone-throwing hooligans,' I said cheerfully. 'A window in the conservatory was broken.'

Guy stopped staring at Adam and glanced round the room, noting the two armchairs pulled up to the fire, the two cups and plates. It was clear that he leapt to conclusions.

'I see,' he said heavily. 'You might have told me the truth in the first place, instead of fobbing me off with... Sorry I burst in. Good night.'

I closed the door behind him and turned to find Adam watching me with a frown.

'Shall we have that coffee now?' I said, returning to my place.

Adam sat quietly, obviously puzzling things over, while I chatted on about my trip to Ilfracombe. Eventually, as though unable to contain himself any longer, he interrupted the flow of my trivialities.

'Why didn't you explain to him?'

'To whom?'

'To Guy, of course. You've let him go off thinking... *Have* you been fobbing him off?'

'Fending him off might be more accurate.'

'What did he mean about...' He stopped abruptly, stirring his coffee with elaborate concentration. 'Sorry, it's none of my business.'

'I don't mind telling you,' I said quietly. 'He more or less said he was in love with me. He may imagine he is—I don't know enough about him to tell. But I made it very clear that I didn't feel the same and when I stopped him from seducing me he got very angry so I told him to leave. That's all there is to it.'

The silence lengthened. I knew that Adam was staring at me, but I kept my gaze on the fire, watching the glowing caves among the coals.

'But he probably came to apologise,' he said at last. 'I would have thought...'

'I know what you thought,' I interrupted. 'But I'm not so naïve that I'm bowled over by good looks and money. I've come to the conclusion that Guy is both spoiled and immature. Would you believe it, he actually offered me mink and diamonds? He must have been watching too many old films. Even Richard...' I paused, flushing.

'Is there any more coffee?' Adam asked, being tactful.

But I had gone too far to stop now. I wanted to tell him the truth about myself and have it done with, before he found out from some other source.

'Richard was more subtle,' I said to the fireplace. 'Too subtle for the sheltered flower that I was. I believed everything he said. He never mentioned marriage, but I assumed that was what he intended, so...'

'Don't, Lyn,' Adam pleaded.

I looked at him squarely, my heart thudding painfully in my throat. 'You might as well know I...was pregnant.' I paused, having said the dreaded word, and then rushed on. 'I had just told Richard when the crash happened. Of course, I lost the baby. And Richard never came near me again. I wrote to him, when I was well enough, but he never came. It seemed like the end of the world... But now I'm grateful to him. He taught me a lot about life... So you see,' I added bitterly, 'Guy had the right idea about me.'

Silently, his eyes full of agony, Adam

reached out and clasped my hand. 'Lyn!' he breathed. 'It doesn't matter. None of it.'

Tears filled my eyes, slid silently down my cheeks. And Adam quietly came to kneel before me, folding his arms about me. We remained like that for some time, simply holding onto each other, and my bitterness gave way to a sense of overwhelming peace. I was glad that Adam knew the truth. Now he could decide for himself what he wanted to do about me.

Leaning away to look at me seriously, he asked, 'Does anyone else know about this?'

'Only the doctors and nurses at the hospital. I suppose it's all down on my medical records. Scalp lacerations. Miscarriage, of three-month...'

'Stop that! It's over and done with. We're going to forget it. Look, I'm off duty all week-end. What would you like to do?'

'I've promised to go up to the Mount. Uncle Jonathon wants me to go to the cove to look for his tunnel.'

'May I come with you?'

I was too full up to speak. I clasped my arms about his neck and held him tightly to me.

* * * *

In the middle of the night, I was woken by the sound of a dog barking. Half asleep, I tumbled out of bed, wondering what was wrong with Smokey, and had reached the door before I remembered that Smokey was dead. But the dog kept barking. It was in the garden.

Worrying about my friend the grey cat, I felt my way along the landing to the window which looked onto the back garden and as I reached it the dog's noise was abruptly choked off. A deathly silence filled the garden. I could see very little in the darkness. Just the vague shape of the trees and a faint light gleaming off the conservatory. But nothing moved.

Shivering, I went back to bed.

* * * *

When Adam called for me the following morning I didn't mention the incident of the night. There was probably a good explanation for the barking dog and it hadn't worried me unduly.

'If we're going down the cliff,' he said,

'you'd better put something warm on. And bring a scarf for your hair. There's a sea-mist this morning.'

'I had noticed,' I replied.

'Yes. Well, we don't want you catching pneumonia. The group practice is overworked as it is.' He was teasing me, more relaxed than I had yet seen him, and as we walked out to the car his arm was about my waist.

Having seen Uncle Jonathon, who showed Adam the letter which he thought was proof of the existence of a tunnel, we went out to the cliff and climbed down the steep path.

Adam went first, holding my hand and saying, 'Be careful. It's slippery...mind that bit...keep away from that edge.'

The mist was so thick that we were halfway down before we could see the sea below us. It was quiet today, small waves gently nudging the base of the unmoving cliff, but there was still the grinding roar of the undertow as the stones rubbed one against another with the backwash of each wave. The tide was not yet at its height, but the smooth stones were wet with the sea-fret that clung round us and my hair felt lank and damp where the scarf didn't cover it.

'We must be crazy,' Adam said as he helped me down the last small drop. 'We explored this place when we were kids.'

'I know,' I replied, 'but I promised Uncle Jonathon I'd have a good look this time.'

We made our way carefully over the uneven stones to the back of the cove, where the sea never reached. The gaunt cliff hung above us, its top shrouded in mist, its feet buried deep in bushes which almost hid the narrow crack in the rock.

'If it's anywhere,' Adam said, indicating the fissure, 'it has to be in there. But as I remember it only goes a few yards and then stops.'

'It seems to. But then I never explored it with a torch. Did you?'

He grinned at me and pulled out the heavy torch he had pushed into his pocket. 'No, I didn't. Come on. And mind these bushes. They're prickly.'

He pushed through the bushes, which were dripping wet, and squeezed into the crevice, with me at his heels. A few feet on, the crack widened and the roof was higher, but it was full of a jumble of rocks and smelled strongly of bird droppings. There were fragments of twigs and moss brought in by nesting birds and laid along a ledge which ran deep into the cave and ended in a pile of boulders fallen from the inside of the cliff. They weren't proper nests and I wondered if the seabirds had been put off the place by the prowling of the grey cat.

The torchlight probed the shadows, but we saw nothing but a solid mass of rocks. Nowhere was there an opening.

'If there ever was a tunnel,' Adam said, 'it's obviously been closed off. Rock-fall probably.'

'Yes, it looks like it,' I agreed, shivering. 'Gosh, Adam, I'm glad you came with me. It's creepy in here.'

He lowered his voice, making it reverberate hollowly around the confined space. 'We are surrounded by the ghosts of dead smugglers,' he said, and put his arm tightly about me. 'Do you remember how Martin used to scare you girls to death whenever he got you in here? You and Melly used to run out screaming.'

'Martin was a horrid boy,' I said primly. 'But I think we secretly enjoyed being frightened.'

I remembered one of those times—myself

about ten, Melly a little dumpling aged eight, Jenny at twelve and the boys both sixteen. But of course Jenny had never come down to the cove with us. She was too terrified of heights to brave the cliff path, which was why Martin, who always tended to be a bully, had tried to drag her with him. She had been screaming hysterically when Adam launched himself at Martin and they had fought until their noses were bloody and Uncle Jonathon had come out to separate them.

Even then, I thought ruefully, Adam had been Jenny's champion. If she had not gone to America...but she *had* gone, and seemed likely to stay away. It was I who stood beside Adam now and his arm about me was strong and possessive.

* * * *

We returned to the house, where Uncle Jonathon was waiting impatiently, surrounded by his beloved weapons collection as he searched in vain through his papers for some clue he had missed.

'I didn't really expect you to find anything,' he said with a sigh. 'But wasn't there some evidence? Some indication...?'

'Nothing at all,' Adam said. 'I'm sorry, Mr Hathersage. It's just a narrow cave. There's a lot of fallen rock lying around. After so many years, whatever clues there might have been have disappeared.'

Uncle Jonathon sadly shook his greying head, stroking his bandaged hand absent-mindedly. Then he began to search through the papers strewn on the desk and produced a photograph.

'This came this morning. There's a letter, too, somewhere.'

Adam took the photograph, glanced at it briefly, and handed it to me. It was a colour picture of my cousin Jenny, sitting on a white fence, her silver-blonde hair blowing to one side, her lovely face alight with laughter. There was a man beside her, a man with curly fair hair, gazing at Jenny with adoration.

I glanced at Adam, but his face was a mask of disinterest.

'Ah, here it is.' Uncle Jonathon discovered the airmail envelope and took out a single sheet of rustling thin paper, reading from it. 'She says, "This is me in Texas. Enjoying myself, as always. I'm staying here with Grant Pearson's family for a long holiday, getting in plenty of riding

and trying not to ruin my figure. Hope you are all well. Love to all the family, including Adam, your loving daughter..." '
He folded the letter, keeping his head bent as though he didn't want us to see his emotion, but his voice had betrayed him. He was missing Jenny terribly.

'Who is Grant Pearson?' I asked, breaking the awkward silence.

'I expect *that* is,' Adam said, flicking the photograph with a casual finger. 'She's never mentioned him before.'

He sounded very certain, as though he read everything which Jenny wrote to her father. Since Uncle Jonathon had not heard my question I touched him on the shoulder and, when he looked up, repeated it.

My uncle shrugged. 'Don't know, Lyn. She never wrote about him before, did she, Adam?'

'Not that I remember,' Adam said.

'She must have lots of friends that we don't know about,' Uncle Jonathon said unhappily, gazing longingly at the photograph of his daughter. Then he put it aside and stood up. 'Are you two staying for lunch?'

Adam and I exchanged glances, silently

agreeing that neither of us wished to stay, and Adam said that we had arranged to have lunch in Ilfracombe and do some shopping, which wasn't entirely true but served its purpose.

We soon turned the lie into a semblance of truth, however, for we did drive into town, lunched in a Chinese restaurant, then Adam bought himself a shirt and I purchased some paint and wallpaper. By the time this was all accomplished I had put aside my fears about Adam and Jenny. He mentioned her only once, and that was to criticise her for her selfishness. She was, he said, so involved in her exciting new life that she seemed to forget how lonely her father might be, and her postcards and brief letters did little to fill the gap.

Without any spoken agreement between us, I found myself preparing a meal for two while Adam set to work on the bigger of the two bedrooms, where I intended to start my redecorations. As I worked in the kitchen I could hear him moving furniture about, putting it all in the centre of the room. He came to ask where he could find dust sheets, and disappeared again with a bucketful of warm water to start soaking the old paper, whistling to himself.

* * * *

We were in the middle of washing-up—a chore which was turned into a pleasure for me by Adam's company—when Uncle Jonathon arrived. He had come to bring me his collection of documents.

'I know you'll take care of them,' he said. 'I'm afraid of what might happen if they're left at the Mount. Lottie's planning so many changes I doubt we'll recognise the place soon.'

Adam and I had discussed my conversation with Lottie, so he knew all about the hotel idea and said now, 'Don't you approve of the plan, Mr Hathersage?'

'I don't,' my uncle said flatly. 'That woman has no right...but what can I do? I had a hard time persuading them not to bother poor old Maude with that central heating business. Lottie's just waiting for the old girl to die. And after that she'll have a go at getting rid of me. There've been hints already.'

'What sort of hints?' I asked worriedly.

'Oh...about the factory. Seems like with the Garden Centre and this hotel business they can't be bothered with making furniture. But if it's necessary I'll buy out James' interest in that and run it on my own. They'd like to see me pensioned off, but I'm not having it.' He paused, massaging his injured hand as if it were aching, and added grimly, 'Anyhow, there's a long way to go before they turn the old place into a tourist trap and they may not find it as easy as they think.'

He was sitting on the sagging settee and now I sat opposite him, leaning forward to study his face.

'Did something happen this afternoon?'

He nodded gloomily. 'They showed me the plans. There's to be a bar, with space for dancing. The sitting-room's to be turned into a restaurant, the dining-room into a resident's lounge. And they want to put a billiard table in my gun room.'

'But what about the weapons collection?' I asked.

Uncle Jonathon grunted. 'That's to go on display in the hall and the bar. Oh, don't worry—they've thought of everything. This time next year you won't know the place.'

'But...does Uncle James agree to all this?' I asked.

'Of course. Rubbing his hands already at the thought of all the profits he'll be raking in. And Martin, too. He's talking about expanding the stables in a year or two.'

I glanced at Adam, who was leaning on the back of the settee, looking as concerned as I felt. He said quietly, 'Change the subject, Lyn. Try to cheer him up.'

It seemed like a good idea. I had never seen Uncle Jonathon so downhearted.

I reached out and touched his knee to attract his attention. 'I've got something to tell you. You know that tunnel...'

'There isn't one,' he said dully. 'Even that has failed.'

I shook my head vigorously. 'Not necessarily. There's an entrance to it in the house.'

My uncle stared at me for a moment in silence, as though he wondered if he had read my lips correctly, then said flatly, 'Where?'

'In Aunt Maude's room. Behind the wardrobe.'

I had his full attention now, and Adam's, and proceeded to tell them of what had happened the night I found Aunt Maude trying to barricade the door of her wardrobe. It was a difficult business. Being totally deaf, Uncle Jonathon missed a word here and there and I had to keep repeating myself until the complicated tale was clear to him.

'You actually saw the stairs?' he said eventually, the light back in his eyes. 'Why didn't you tell me?'

'You were in hospital. I didn't want to tell anyone else. I was waiting to see you alone, but I think we can trust Adam. You see, Aunt Maude swore me to secrecy.'

'I should think so!' my uncle exclaimed, and turned to Adam, who by this time was sitting beside him. 'You won't mention this, will you?'

'Certainly not,' Adam said solemnly.

Uncle Jonathon was excited now. 'It will be tricky getting in there without disturbing Aunt Maude,' he said. 'But leave it to me. I'll wait for my moment.' His fist pounded his knee and his brown face broke into a grin. 'We won't tell the others until I've looked at it. I don't suppose you saw where it went to?'

'I was busy with Aunt Maude,' I said.

'Oh, yes, of course. But I was right, wasn't I?'

We both agreed that it certainly looked that way, and Uncle Jonathon took his leave with a new sprightly swing to his limping walk.

* * * *

'That was a life-saver,' Adam said approvingly. 'He was really down in the dumps, wasn't he?'

'Yes, he was. But that blood-poisoning can't have helped any.' I picked up the package of papers and held them carefully. 'I consider myself very honoured to be trusted with these. Uncle Jonathon regards them as the family treasure. These and his beloved weapons... Oh, Adam, I do hope they aren't going to ruin the Mount.'

'So do I, but something had to be done. This last few years the repair bills have had them worried to death. If it hadn't been for Lottie, they might have had to sell the Mount.'

'Yes...' I said thoughtfully. 'But I wonder what she's getting out of it.'

'She's a business woman. A hotel in this area is good business.'

'Do you think that's why she married Uncle James?'

Adam laughed, lounging back on the settee. 'I couldn't begin to speculate about that. Women are a mystery to me.'

'H'm. That's what *you* say.' I moved away, putting the family documents into the sideboard, and turned to find Adam regarding me seriously.

'You really care about the Mount, don't you? I mean, if Jonathon does find his tunnel it will really give you a kick.'

'Of course it will. A real smugglers' tunnel—where my ancestors once walked... I can't wait to see it. I hope he does find it.'

'It's a pity that...' He paused in mid-sentence and the silence lengthened until I prompted, ' "A pity that" what?'

'That Jenny couldn't have been like you,' Adam said. 'It would have meant a lot to Jonathon if his daughter had shared his interest.'

'I know.' Why, why did he have to mention Jenny just then, when I had forgotten my suspicions and was beginning to think that Adam and I had something special growing between us?

He leapt up from the settee, a picture

of bounding energy. 'Well, what about that wallpaper? It shouldn't take us long to finish stripping. And the walls are in good condition.'

'They should be. My father had the whole cottage done over by experts a few years ago. He didn't want Gran to have to worry about repairs.'

'Shall we get on with it, then?'

My enthusiasm did not match his, but I didn't relish the thought of a quiet evening with Jenny as an unseen third in my mind. So we stripped wallpaper, chatting and laughing until once more I put my beautiful cousin out of my thoughts. She was in America, with someone named Grant Pearson. And Adam was here, with me.

* * * *

It was very late when at last I went to bed, warm in the memory of that last quiet half hour sipping hot chocolate by the fire, my head on Adam's shoulder, our lips meeting occasionally. I was so happy that I sang to myself as I undressed.

But when I was on the verge of sleep I heard again the sound which had disturbed me the previous night—a dog, barking a warning in the garden. Once more I ran to the landing window, and, as I reached it the barking stopped abruptly.

One incident like that was puzzling, but only slightly so. But two...two so exactly alike. Exactly as Smokey must have sounded that night when he was killed. A dog barking. Grabbed and silenced.

My heart was thudding with a fear which bordered on panic. Was I hearing a ghost? Had Smokey come back to haunt the garden?

And then a light caught my eye, flickering through the yew trees of the churchyard. A round red light, and then another, moving in an uneven line until they went out of my sight at the side of the cottage.

I went back to my room and in the darkness knelt on my bed to draw aside the curtain. This window looked into one corner of the churchyard. The lights were still there, gleaming a dull red and moving away. And then they were gone, as if a hand had snapped a switch.

Wandering red lights in a churchyard, and a ghostly dog barking... I did not sleep well that night.

CHAPTER SEVEN

By morning, the whole village was buzzing with the news of another haunting at the church. A young courting couple had seen the lights and so had a man driving home from a Masonic meeting. Of course, everyone had known for a long time that the church was haunted. Mr Tregannon, the verger, said that he, for one, wouldn't go near the churchyard after dark.

All this news was imparted to me by Adam when he arrived, as promised, to help me paint the bedroom. He was wearing an ancient sweater faded from many washings, and the ghost story seemed to amuse him.

'These things break out now and then,' he said, 'especially at the start of the tourist season. It makes good telling for the visitors.'

'You mean,' I said flatly, 'you don't believe it.'

'No, of course I don't. What's the matter, Lyn? You look a bit peaky. Didn't you sleep well?'

'As a matter of fact, I didn't. I saw those lights, too. And I also heard a dog's barking that was suddenly choked off.'

'A dog?' Adam said. 'Where?'

'It sounded to be in the garden. Like Smokey... And don't look at me like that! I'm not imagining things.'

'Lyn,' he said patiently, taking me by the shoulders and looking deep into my eyes. 'All these things have a rational explanation. Did you ever meet anybody who ever saw a ghost?'

'You're looking at one now. Oh, it was a long time ago when I was a child, and children are known to be more psychic, but I didn't imagine it and there was no other explanation. So these lights and things...well, I don't know what they are. *You* explain it.'

Adam was silent for a while, struggling with his scepticism. 'I don't know,' he said eventually. 'But look...you shouldn't stay here alone any more. I wish you'd move back to the Mount and...'

'No. This is my home. I'm not frightened. After all, ghosts never hurt anybody... Adam, I hope you don't think I'm going crazy.'

'Of course I don't. You're the most rational person I know, but...'

'But what?'

'Nothing. Only I want you to tell me if you see or hear anything else.'

'Yes, doctor.'

His lips compressed angrily and his green eyes snapped at me. 'Damn it, Lyn, can't I even worry about you a little? This cottage is miles from anywhere except the Mount, and that's a good ten minutes walk. When I think about you all alone here every night... What would you do if something happened? Suppose someone broke in?'

'I'll keep a poker under my pillow,' I said.

Exasperated, Adam ran a hand through his red hair, leaving it standing on end in a comical way. 'Honestly, Lyn, you're the most... Oh, I give up.' He pulled me to him and kissed me very thoroughly, his arms holding me tight against him. My own arms found their way around him and when he let me go I was laughing from sheer joy. 'Well, really, Doctor Taylor!' I teased. 'And you a sworn woman-hater.'

'You,' Adam said severely, 'have been listening to malicious gossip.'

* * * *

I had looked forward to spending another whole day with Adam, but it was not to be. We had hardly made a start on the painting when Dr Taylor, Senior, arrived with the news that a special patient of Adam's was very ill and asking for him.

'I shall have to go,' Adam said ruefully, cleaning his hands on a rag. 'This old man is very particular and seems to think I have some extra magic. I could refuse to go, but...'

'Of course you couldn't,' I told him. 'If someone is ill and wants you...I do understand, Adam. I hope he'll be all right.'

'Thank you, Lyn.' He kissed me then, and turned to the door. 'Shall I come back when I've seen what's wrong?'

'If you want to.'

'I want to,' he said definitely. 'But I don't know how long I shall be. One never knows what complications may arise. So if I don't come, you'll know why.' He smiled at me as he opened the door. 'You may regret getting involved with a doctor. Imagine what it must be like getting married to one! 'Bye, Lyn.'

And he left me wondering what it would be like to be married, not just to any doctor, but to Adam Taylor. I didn't think the upsets of a GP's life would worry me if I was waiting for Adam, there to comfort and cheer him when he came home tired and worried. He really cared about people. Any woman ought to be proud to be his wife.

Remembering my brief flirtation with Guy Breder, I thought that I must have been mad. There was no doubt now in my mind which of the two men I preferred. It was Adam every time. In a few short weeks I had come to care for him in a way I had never imagined was possible.

* * * *

I was busy painting the window-frame, with the sun warm on my arms, when I saw Guy's red Jaguar nose out from the drive of Hathercombe Mount. It pulled up opposite the cottage gate and I hoped he was not coming to call on me. But it was Melly who emerged from the far side of the car and waved at me.

Her hair was freshly washed and set

and she was wearing a scarlet coat cut on slimming lines. Obviously she had gone to great trouble over her appearance.

'Hello,' she called. 'You look busy. How are you?'

'Fine,' I replied. 'And where are you off to, all dolled up?'

Even from this distance I could see her blush as she answered with throw-away casualness, 'Oh, Guy and I are going out for the day. There's an *atmosphere* at the Mount. Dad and Uncle Jonathon must have had words. So we're getting out of their way. See you, Lyn. Have fun.'

They drove off, and I wondered whose idea it had been to stop and let me know they were going out together. Melly's—as a show of triumph? Or Guy's—for spite, trying to make me regret my treatment of him? But my concern was for Melly. She was an innocent in the ways of the world, as I had been before I met Richard. I hoped that Guy wouldn't hurt her. Her affections, once aroused, were apt to be traumatic. She clung like a leech. Her joy was mountain-high, her depressions deep as the deepest coal mine. There were no half-measures with Melly. Poor, poor Melly.

* * * *

It was nine o'clock that evening when Adam came back. He looked strained and pale and I understood why when he told me that his patient had been taken to hospital, where he had died. Since there were no sons or daughters, Adam had taken the man's wife home and stayed with her until the neighbours returned from a day out and promised to look after the old lady for a few days.

'I couldn't leave her,' Adam said. 'Poor old girl. Her husband was all she had. But the neighbours seem like nice people. They'll help her over the worst stages... I'm sorry it took so long, Lyn.'

'Don't be,' I said quietly. 'I'm glad you cared enough to keep her company.'

He pulled me into his arms and held me there, my face against his throat, where I could feel the steady pulse beating. 'I'm glad you understand,' he said. 'It means a lot to me.'

* * * *

The dog, ghost or not, did bark again

that night. I lay in bed and listened to it. It seemed to go on for much longer than it had done previously, but it eventually stopped and I settled back to sleep, only to be shocked awake by three loud crashes, one after another. I sat up in bed, shivering, then called back my fleeing courage and got up, pulling my dressing-gown round me.

Switching on lights as I went, until the cottage was brilliant as a Christmas tree, I made my way to the kitchen and fearfully opened the back door. The shaft of light in the conservatory showed me three more broken panes of glass. Two of the plants had been upset and lay in spilling soil, their pots broken, amid a glitter of shattered glass.

I stood staring at the mess, my heart hammering painfully, and nearly hit the ceiling when a loud banging sounded on the front door. Closing the back door, I went through to the sitting-room.

'Who's there?' I called.

There was no reply.

I glanced at the clock on the mantelpiece above the dead grey ashes of the fire. It was 2.10 a.m exactly.

'Who is it?' I demanded, my voice rising

in panic, and at that moment I heard the conservatory door crash open.

My back to the bolted front door, I stood stiffened in fear for a moment, remembering that I had unlocked the back door. I was shaking now and went to take the poker from the hearth before venturing into the kitchen.

Nothing stirred. Everything was silent. I put off the kitchen light, pulled the curtain aside, but when my eyes had adjusted to the darkness I could see only the shape of the conservatory, the door wide open now. I didn't dare to go out there. I locked the back door securely and went to sit on the settee, gripping the poker between my hands. Nothing else happened. When my screaming nerves had quietened I went back to bed.

* * * *

'Poltergeists?' Uncle James said sceptically. 'Now really, Lynda, this is too much. Just because the village is seething with ghost stories... Your nerves are overwrought, my dear.'

I had gone to the Mount hoping for help, hoping to see Uncle Jonathon. But he had gone to the factory and so I had told my tale to Uncle James and Lottie, in the room set aside as an office.

'I can't prove that I heard the dog,' I said, 'or that I saw lights and heard doors banging, but there are four broken panes of glass in my conservatory.'

'Four? You said three.'

'Yes. One was smashed on Friday night. That was done by some boys. Adam saw them running away. But...'

'Ah well. There's your answer. Hooliganism. It's a modern disease.'

Lottie spoke then for the first time, her voice soft, her eyes full of sympathy. 'That is true, James. But I do think we should invite Lynda to stay with us for a while. The poor girl has obviously been badly frightened.'

'Oh, yes,' said Uncle James, hugging his great paunch, his little piggy eyes expressing his low opinion of me. 'Of course she may come, if she wishes. You're welcome, Lynda. But please don't start seeing ghosts here.'

I felt so angry that I daren't reply to that remark. I had never liked Uncle James much and his attitude now did not improve my opinion of him.

'Thank you,' I said. 'If you can just spare me a bed...I shall stay at the cottage during the day.'

* * * *

So it was arranged. I was to sleep at the Mount temporarily. Meanwhile I called the police station and a constable came out and had a look round the cottage, shook his head over the broken glass and promised to 'look into it'. He found nothing else.

It seemed that my 'ghost' would go on the 'unsolved' file along with the mystery of who had carried Gran into the conservatory and left a muddy footprint.

* * * *

During the afternoon, Melly arrived. Her hair still looked quite pretty, but the effect was marred by the evidences of pink ointment on her face and by the terribly baggy clothes she wore.

She looked with interest at the empty squares in the conservatory.

'Those boys in the village get rowdier every year,' she remarked. 'Lottie told me all about it. I expect they're just trying to frighten you. After all, you *are* a newcomer.'

'You think it was a gang of boys who made those noises, too?' I asked.

My cousin shrugged. 'Why not? Martin says if you'd gone outside and shouted at them they'd have left you alone... Anyway, so you're coming back to the Mount?'

'Only to sleep. For a few nights. Do you mind?'

'That all depends. I mean...you won't start setting your cap at Guy again, will you?'

'Setting my cap?' I exclaimed.

'Yes...well...you know what I mean. Going riding with him, and then entertaining him here—alone.'

'I assure you,' I said. 'It wouldn't worry me if I never saw Guy again.'

My voice must have carried conviction, for Melly immediately brightened and then, just as suddenly, looked thoughtful.

'Adam, is it?' she asked. 'Of course, you know about him and Jenny, don't you?'

'I know he used to be fond of her,' I replied coolly. 'But that was five years ago. Jenny is thousands of miles away. And Adam doesn't appear to be languishing with unrequited love, not as far as I can see. Anyway, a man like Adam is bound to have known other women. I've known other young men, too.'

'Yes, but Adam...' She paused, biting her red lip. 'Oh well, I suppose you know better than I do. You'll just have to hope that Jenny never comes back.'

I was getting sick of the sound of that name. Everybody seemed to know what had happened between Jenny and Adam—everyone except me. And I wanted to know. Or did I?... Yes, I did, I told myself angrily. Whatever it was, it was in the past and didn't worry me. I was almost sure that Adam loved me—as sure as I ever could be until he actually said so.

* * * *

I slept peacefully that night, in the room near Aunt Maude's. I went to see the old lady, but she thought I was Sonja, the lovely Swedish girl who had married Uncle Jonathon and died a few years after Jenny was born. My great-aunt's memory was really haywire, for I had seen the portrait of Sonja which hung in the gallery and I bore not the slightest resemblance to it.

I didn't have breakfast at the Mount. A bed was all I had asked for and a bed was all I intended to take. In my own way, I was as proud and stubborn as the other Hathersages. So I returned to the cottage through a rainstorm, wondering what I would find.

There had been no more breakages, but the rain poured in through the gaps in the conservatory and as I opened the kitchen door I heard a rustling among some newspapers in the corner. The grey cat was there, bristling with animosity. It must have come in through one of the empty window-spaces and been unable to get out. This was hardly surprising, I realised, seeing now that I was close to it that its belly was distended with young. The cat was a female and heavily pregnant.

She wouldn't come near me. When I tried to touch her she spat and leapt to one side, less agile now because of her awkward body, though she made no attempt to scratch me. I put out a big dish of milk, leaving it on the earthenware tiles, and went to collect all the scraps of food I had left. Coming back cautiously, I found the cat lapping greedily at the milk. She crouched low, whiskers twitching, great yellow eyes full of wariness, but she didn't move away as I put the plate of scraps on the floor, talking softly the whole time.

Stepping past the cat, I opened the conservatory door and went across to the shed for some sticks. When I returned, the cat was in the doorway, torn between braving the cold and the rain or staying where there was food and a chance of incarceration. I left the door wide open, giving her an escape route, and went into the kitchen, from where I watched the cat come back and begin wolfing the scraps. I felt absurdly pleased to have been given even that small amount of trust.

* * * *

As I was lighting the fire, Martin walked in through the front door without knocking and stood dripping on the doormat, his curly hair protected by a cloth cap.

'Is Uncle Jonathon with you?' he asked.

'With me? No, of course not. I've only been here twenty minutes. He was still in bed when I left.'

'Did you see him?'

'Not this morning. But I assumed he...'

'Yes, we all thought he was in his room, only when Melly went to take him a cup of tea he wasn't there. Nobody's seen him since last night. We wondered if he walked down here with you.'

'No. He didn't. Have you tried the factory?'

'He wouldn't have gone there without breakfast. Oh...I suppose it's worth a try. He's been flitting about all over the place these last few days. And there's another funny thing—somebody ripped the telephone cord out of the wall last night. And Lottie swears Uncle Jonathon did that. He's trying to delay the plans for the hotel. He called the builders and told them not to come, you know. Held us up for over a month.'

'Uncle Jonathon?' I cried. 'Oh, I don't believe it. Did he say it was him?'

'No, but it must have been. Dad's absolutely livid. And now the silly old coot's gone missing.'

I straightened up, furious. 'Don't you talk about Uncle Jonathon like that!'

Martin's ruddy face wore a truculent expression. 'Well, how do you expect us to feel? He's just doing it to annoy us. Anybody would think *he* owned the Mount instead of Dad. He's lucky Dad's let him stay so long.'

'Oh, Martin!' I cried. 'How *can* you? You'd better get out of here before I throw something.'

I was in such a temper that I broke three matches before I got one to light and held it to the papers in the grate, watching as the flames licked up around the sticks and small coals. It was awful of Martin to talk about Uncle Jonathon that way, I thought. Life had been very unfair to my favourite uncle. Deaf and crippled; his beautiful young wife taken from him after a few years of marriage; the daughter on whom he doted leaving him to seek a life of glamour. Even the house he loved had been denied him by the will of my autocratic grandfather, and now his elder brother was trying to turn that house into a money-making enterprise. Oh yes, it was totally unfair.

Putting my energetic feelings to good purpose, I cleaned out the sitting-room and was relaxing with a cup of coffee, feeling calmer, when a car drew up outside. From the window, I saw Adam striding down the path.

'I was near here on a call,' he said.

'Thought I'd look in and see how you were.'

He had time for a quick coffee, he said, and followed me into the kitchen after taking off his raincoat. I told him that I was sleeping at the Mount, and why, and warned him that he had better not say 'I told you so'.

'I promise I won't,' he said as we returned to the sitting-room. 'But how do you feel about me spending a night here—while you're at the Mount, of course. If it is hooligans...' He stopped talking and took hold of me, his hands cold on either side of my face as he bent to kiss me. 'I've missed you. I'd have been up to see you last night except that I was on call. But I'm free tonight. What shall we do?'

'Anything you like,' I said happily, sliding my arms round him. 'Anything at all.'

He tilted my face up to his and smiled into my eyes until his nearness drove his face out of focus and his mouth was on mine, tender and sweet.

And then someone knocked on the door.

'Some people have a lousy sense of timing,' Adam said dourly as I crossed the room.

The caller was Martin, pale-faced and looking sick.

'Lyn...' he got out. 'Adam...' He came inside the cottage, staring from me to Adam and back again.

My heart, which a moment before had been crazy with joy, began to thud with fear.

'Martin,' Adam said sternly. 'What's wrong? Look, man, come and sit down.'

'I can't,' Martin said. 'I've got to get back. They...they found Uncle Jonathon. A mile down the coast. He's dead, Lyn. Drowned.'

CHAPTER EIGHT

I went back to the Mount with Martin and was there when the police came to make their enquiries. It was established that Uncle Jonathon had gone to bed as usual, but his movements after that were a mystery. All the evidence was trotted out—the cancellation of the builders; the disconnected phone; Uncle Jonathon's annoyance about the hotel plan; his loneliness; his recent depression. And then someone mentioned his search for a smugglers' tunnel.

The cliff path was examined and a piece found to be broken off the edge, as though it might have given way under someone's weight. The police appeared to think that Uncle Jonathon had committed suicide.

'He couldn't have done!' I protested to the gathered assembly. 'He was afraid of the cliff. He told me so. He couldn't bear heights. That's true, isn't it, Uncle James?'

My uncle frowned. 'He used to be. The subject hasn't come up for years. Perhaps he knew that he would fall. Perhaps he wanted to. He has been behaving most irrationally.'

A loud sob came from Melly as she dissolved again into the noisy tears she had indulged in ever since the news came. I saw Guy bend over her solicitously.

As the police were leaving, Lottie drew me aside and asked me if I would stay at the Mount for the day. Clearly Melly was going to need to rest and Mrs Porter could not be expected to cope with the demands of the house and of Aunt Maude on her own. Life, said Lottie, tritely, had to go on, and there were business matters which must be dealt with, and since I was not otherwise employed...

'Of course I'll stay,' I replied.

Melly went to lie down and remained in her room for the rest of the day. My time was spent in the kitchen, when I was not running up and down stairs in response to Aunt Maude's frequent summonses from her electric bell. The old lady had not been told about the tragedy, though I wondered if she would notice Uncle Jonathon's absence. He and Uncle James were the only members of the family she unfailingly recognised.

'I don't know how Melly manages,' I said when we gathered for lunch. 'I'm exhausted already. Wouldn't it be more sensible to have Aunt Maude downstairs? Or even employ a nurse?'

The silence reminded me of the time when I had confessed to leaving the old lady's door unlocked. Once again I was the interloper, interfering.

'My dear Lynda,' Uncle James said in a heavily patient tone. 'There are no suitable rooms downstairs. Are you suggesting that we should make alterations which would be useless after the short time Aunt Maude has left? And as for a nurse!... Have you any idea how much such a person would ask as a wage? Aunt Maude is very fit. She has her bell to hand, and she is never left alone for more than an hour at a time.'

'But in an hour—even in a few minutes... she might fall. Anything could happen.'

My uncle's deep-set eyes, almost hidden by folds of flesh, regarded me unblinkingly. 'It might. That's true. But she has lived a very long life, if one can call it living. This may sound callous, but death could only be a release for her.'

It did sound callous. It *was* callous. They were prepared to spend no end of money on their fancy plans, but when it came to preserving the life of an old lady... Obviously she was in their way. As Uncle Jonathon had been.

A terrible suspicion began to form in my mind. I did not believe that Uncle Jonathon had killed himself. I did not believe that he had accidentally fallen from the cliff path. There had been angry 'words' between the brothers. Melly had said so. And Uncle Jonathon had been making a nuisance of himself, delaying the plans of his ambitious brother. The conclusion was so awful that it made me feel sick.

I excused myself and left the table.

★ ★ ★ ★

Adam came after his evening surgery and was shown into the long sitting-room where I sat with Uncle James and Martin. I thought he had come to see me, but his first words were:

'Has anybody contacted Jenny?'

'I did,' Uncle James said. 'I eventually got through to this ranch place where she's staying. She said she would leave as soon as possible.'

'She's coming?' Adam asked.

'Naturally,' my uncle replied.

Martin stirred in his chair, saying bitterly, 'Even she couldn't stay away now. Though it won't do Uncle Jonathon any good.'

'She wasn't to know this would happen!' Adam said angrily. 'Lyn, can I speak to you in private?'

Numbly, I left my chair. So Jenny was coming home. Jenny, whom Adam was still defending.

We made our way to the library, which smelled of leather and beeswax and was soon to be the reading-room of Hathercombe Hotel.

'Have you thought about what I suggested?' Adam asked as he closed the door behind him.

I stared at him blankly, not understanding.

'About my sleeping at the cottage,' he explained.

'Oh...that. No, I haven't given it another thought. Does it matter now?'

'Well of course it matters. You want to be able to live there again, don't you? And I'd like to find out for myself what's going on. Hasn't it occurred to you that someone might have tried to frighten you away?'

'Why should they?'

'I don't know. But remember what happened to your grandmother and Smokey. None of this ghost business started until you had gone back to the cottage.'

'How do you know? There was no one there to see or hear it.'

'All the same,' Adam said, 'I'd like to find out for myself. So may I please have the key?'

It was in my handbag in the sitting-room. I fetched it and brought it back to him.

'You'll need some clean sheets,' I said.

'I'll come back with you and...'

'No you won't. I'll doss down on the settee. You get an early night. You look as though you need it.'

'Adam...you will be careful, won't you?'

He took me in his arms, holding me closely. 'Of course I will. Don't you worry. I'll see you tomorrow.'

* * * *

Taking his advice, I went to bed early. My grief over Uncle Jonathon and my concern for Adam warred in my mind but were overcome by the physical tiredness of the day. I slept deeply and dreamlessly.

It was seven-thirty when I woke, a bright spring morning in early April. Mrs Porter and Melly were already beginning to prepare breakfast, my cousin looking wan and big-eyed, still ready to burst into tears at the slightest provocation.

I decided to walk down to the cottage and see if Adam had had any trouble during the night. His car was parked on the verge just inside the driveway, so I knew he must still be there, but the front door was locked and there was no answer to my knocking. I walked round to the back of the cottage. The door to the conservatory was open and my cat stood by it. When she saw me, she mewed plaintively.

'In a minute,' I said. 'I'll get you some food in a minute.'

Knocking loudly on the kitchen door, I peered through the window. There was no sign of life in the cottage, though Adam would surely not have left without his car. Worried now, I tried the door, which opened beneath my hand.

'Adam?' I called.

In reply there came a muffled groan.

I found him lying at the foot of the stairs. As I ran to him he stirred and put a hand to his head, where dried blood matted his chestnut hair.

'Adam!' I knelt beside him, cradling his head on my lap. 'Adam, darling, are you all right?'

His eyes looked dazedly up at me. 'I think so... God ! My head!'

'What happened?' I asked frantically.

'I...I don't remember. I was asleep. On the settee. I thought I heard something and...' He closed his eyes. 'That's all.'

I looked up at the stairs, at the lethal low beam spanning them. 'Did you go upstairs? To the bathroom? That beam...'

'I don't know,' he groaned, struggling to sit up. I put my arm under him and helped him get to his feet.

'Adam!' I said urgently. 'When you woke up...was it dark?'

'As pitch. Early hours, I think.'

'Then we must get you straight to hospital. You've been unconscious for hours. Concussion...'

He looked at me with green eyes full of pain. 'Yes, you're right, Lyn. Can you drive?'

I could, and did, delivering him to the Casualty Ward at Ilfracombe, where I was eventually told that he would be kept in under observation for a day or two. Bumps on the head were always potentially dangerous, especially when the patient had been unconscious.

The nurses were reassuring, but I was very worried as I drove Adam's car back to Hathercombe and explained to his father what had happened.

'I don't suppose there's any call to worry,' Doctor Taylor said, smiling at me with green eyes exactly like his son's. 'Anyway, he's in the right place. Serve him right for tangling with ghosts, eh?'

'I just wish he could remember what

happened,' I said. 'He may have caught his head on that beam, but...'

'Oh, he'll remember. Give him a few days. I don't see what else it could have been, do you?'

I had some wild ideas about malignant spirits, but didn't like to express them.

Back at the cottage, I had a look at the beam across the stairs and found a smear of blood there. Adam must have been to the bathroom in the dark and forgotten about the beam. I was glad to be sure of that.

* * * *

The coroner's verdict on Uncle Jonathon was 'accidental death'. He said there was no proof of intention to commit suicide and I think we were all relieved that that stigma had been removed.

My uncle was brought home on the Thursday morning, to lie in the gun room as had long been the custom. The shining coffin stood on three trestles draped in black and the darkened room was kept lit by candles in twin silver candelabra. Mrs Porter told me that she had seen this done four times in her life—for my grandfather, for Aunt Nora, Uncle James' first wife; and for Sonja, whose husband now lay in the same place. It was a family tradition, old-fashioned, perhaps, but entirely suitable for Uncle Jonathon, who had believed so strongly in tradition. His last hours in the house would be spent in his beloved gun room.

⋆ ⋆ ⋆ ⋆

There was an air of intense expectancy in the Mount. We were waiting for Jenny, who would have to arrive that day if she were to attend the funeral. But the evening meal-time came and went with no sign of her.

We were all gathered in the sitting-room, while outside black clouds rushed in from the Atlantic, bringing a raging storm. Thunder and lightning split the quietness and lights were put on, the curtains drawn against the furore outside. And then Melly, peering out of the window as she had done on and off all day, suddenly shrieked.

'There's a taxi. It's her. It's Jenny!'

She bounced out of the room. I heard the front door open, heard the rain beating down on the terrace, and then Melly exclaiming, 'Oh, Jen. Jen! It's lovely to have you home.'

Uncle James went to the door. 'My dear,' he said, and I saw Jenny come to give him her hands. 'We are all very sorry that this should be such a sad homecoming for you. It's been a great shock to us all. You must be sure that we shall do everything possible to help you... You look tired.'

'I am tired.' She was drawn into the room and stood looking dazedly at us all, tall and slender, a mane of shining ash-blonde hair cascading to the shoulders of her black coat. Her lovely face was tanned but strained and her great violet eyes were shadowed.

Martin went to welcome her home, his lips briefly brushing her temple, and then I approached her. It was a moment before Jenny recognised me.

'Lyn...of course, Dad wrote and told me you were here. I'm glad to see you.'

Lottie was introduced, and then Guy, who stared at Jenny in the way men do stare at a stunningly beautiful woman. There was a glint of that same look in Martin's eyes, despite the fact that he disliked Jenny. She didn't seem to notice, but I saw Melly's lips compress and her eyes were suddenly dark pools of anguish.

'You must have been travelling for a long time,' Lottie said.

'A day and a half,' Jenny replied.

'Your room's all ready,' Melly put in. 'We've put hot bottles in the bed, though we've got central heating now. Shall I get you some food?'

'Oh, no.' Jenny looked as though the very thought of food made her feel ill. 'No, I'm not hungry, Melly. Just dreadfully tired.' She turned to Uncle James. 'What time is the funeral?'

'Eleven o'clock. Everything has been arranged. Your father...is in the gun room, of course. The coffin is closed. We thought it best.'

'Yes,' Jenny said faintly. 'I understand. But I'd like to go and...'

'Shall I come with you?' Melly asked.

Jenny smiled a little, as if touched by this thoughtfulness, but she said, 'No, thank you, Melly. I'm all right.'

Her composure was impressive as she walked across the hall, her heels clicking on the stone mosaic, long shapely legs moving gracefully beneath the short coat.

‘Poor Jenny,’ Melly said, choking back tears. ‘Shall we take her cases up, Lyn? We could unpack for her.’

We did so. Jenny had brought two large suitcases and an overnight bag, the contents of which were soon dispersed in the cupboards and drawers of the room prepared for her. Her clothes were all expensive and elegant. Melly drew the curtains, switched on the bedside light, checked the radiator...

‘Now she can come straight to bed,’ she said. ‘She’ll feel better after a good night’s sleep.’

We returned to the stairs, from where I saw Adam crossing the hall, having come in by the back door. I had not known he was coming out of hospital and was about to call out to him, overjoyed to see him, when Jenny’s voice called his name and he stopped dead, turning slowly as she appeared from the corridor.

‘Adam!’ she said again, her voice low and husky. ‘Oh, Adam, I knew you would come. You’ve kept your promise. You *have* waited for me, Adam...’

Through a misty veil I saw her being clasped in his arms, his head bent low over her pale hair. And part of me died.

I turned away, unable to face the two of them together, and saw the expression of sympathy in Melly's eyes.

'I'm sorry, Lyn,' she breathed. 'But I did try to warn you.'

Reaching out, I pulled her with me, out of sight and hearing of the two in the hall.

'Don't tell him,' I said in a low voice. 'Don't let him know that I saw. I'd rather hear it from him. He'll tell me about it. He'll have to. Melly...they were in love, weren't they?'

She nodded sadly. 'Adam's been crazy about Jenny all his life. When they were both in London they saw each other all the time. I don't know what happened after that—why she went away. He would never say. But...you heard what she said. He must have promised to wait for her. That's why he never bothered with girl-friends. He was waiting for Jenny.'

I turned away, my eyes streaming, hiding my face against the wall.

'Don't, Lyn.' Melly's hand came on my arm. 'Please don't. Look, why don't you go up to your room? I'll tell them you had a raging headache and decided to go to bed.'

I nodded agreement. I couldn't speak. My throat was thick with tears and my whole body hurt. I stumbled along the corridor and into my own room, flinging myself down onto the bed and letting the pain have its way with me. And outside the lightning flared and the thunder rolled, fitting accompaniment for a breaking heart.

CHAPTER NINE

The hearse arrived at ten-thirty and the coffin was put carefully into it. We were going to walk behind it for the short distance to church, through a morning that was fragrant after the storm. The trees and hedges were in full leaf at last, making the world green again.

Jenny, looking fragile and lovely with a black hat setting off her pale hair and tragic face, was to walk with Uncle James. Behind them, Martin and Lottie, followed by Guy with Melly and myself. Then at the last minute Adam arrived and was instructed by Uncle James to walk beside me.

'Are you all right?' he asked anxiously. 'Last night Melly said...'

'Oh, yes, I did feel awful. Delayed reaction, I suppose. How are *you* feeling?'

'Much better, though I've been told not to go back to work until after the holiday.'

'Holiday?... Oh, of course. Good Friday, isn't it? Nothing very good about today, though.'

'No, there isn't.' Gravely, he offered me his arm and we walked in silence behind the others.

* * * *

The funeral was as saddening as all of those occasions. Uncle Jonathon was laid to rest beside his wife, not far from the grave where, so recently, Gran had been buried, and there followed one of those awful post-funeral buffet lunches at the Mount, to which a good many people had been invited—friends from the district and workers from the factory.

I heard Jenny discussing the future of the factory, of which half now belonged to her, with Uncle James, though I only caught part of the conversation.

'...neither do I, Uncle James. I haven't the first idea about business. But would anybody want to buy it? It's only a cottage industry, after all.'

Disgusted, I moved away. Soon, I thought, there would be nothing left of the things Uncle Jonathon had loved.

The next time I saw Jenny she was with Adam, clinging to his arm and looking up into his face, talking intently. Since Adam was totally engrossed in her I again turned away, picking up a load of dirty dishes and taking them to the kitchen, where I remained, helping Mrs Porter with the endless washing-up. I felt sick and miserable, wishing time and again that I had heeded the warning signs and kept my emotions in check. Perhaps if Jenny had never come back...but she *was* back, and it was just as well. Even in absence she would have stood between us. Now Adam needn't settle for second-best. He had the girl he really wanted.

As I had done once before, I took my things and quietly left the Mount. Ghosts or not, I preferred to be at the cottage. At least there I would not be obliged to watch Jenny meeting Adam.

★ ★ ★ ★

The garden was rampant with weeds and since it was a lovely day, I changed from my black dress into an old jumper and faded jeans, preparing to do some gardening. Remembering Jenny's fairy-princess loveliness, I stared in the mirror, deliberately pulling back my hair to expose the disfiguring scar. It was fading from red to pink, but even when it had turned white it would look ugly. My features were irregular, my eyes that odd shade of golden-brown, and beside Jenny's pale-blonde mane my own hair looked merely mousy. I had always envied Jenny, but never more so than now. Perhaps if I had been tall and beautiful I might have made Adam forget her, but it was obvious that his feelings for her had never died.

Engrossed in bitter thoughts, I pulled weeds from beneath the budding lilac in the front garden, tossing them onto the path behind me. After a while, the grey cat came to sit on the path, basking in the tepid April sunlight. Then the gate clicked and I looked up to find Adam standing there, tall and straight in his dark suit and black tie. 'What happened?' he asked.

'Why did you suddenly leave?'

'It wasn't sudden. I finished what I was doing and came away. I always feel...superfluous at the Mount.'

'But...you'll go back tonight, won't you? You can't stay here alone. I still can't remember what happened the night I was here.'

'You crashed into that low beam. I found blood on it. A blow like that can blot out the few minutes before it happened, can't it?'

'I suppose so.' He still sounded doubtful. 'May I have a look at it?'

'There's nothing to see. You didn't think I'd have left dried blood on it, did you? No, I washed it off. And I'm going to stay.' I made the statement in a firm tone, making a stand as mistress of my own life.

Adam didn't reply. He walked slowly down the path and across the straggly grass until he stood beside me as I knelt to tussle with a dandelion root.

'What's Jenny going to do?' I asked.

'I don't think she knows yet. This has all been very unsettling for her. Lyn...I don't know what you're thinking, but I've got to be honest with you...I'm not sure how I feel about Jenny. Seeing her again... She's terribly upset about her father. And she's all alone now. She has no one. Even if I wanted to, I couldn't desert her now. She needs me.'

Jenny all alone? I thought bitterly. When she had Uncle James and Martin and Melly, and all her friends in the States?

'You must do what you want to do,' I said, keeping my head lowered over the mud and weeds. 'You don't have to explain yourself to me.'

'But I want you to understand. Before Jenny left for America, the last thing I said to her was that if she changed her mind and wanted to come back, I would be here.'

'Five years ago,' I muttered. 'You must love her very much.'

'Lyn!' He pulled me up, made me look at him. His face was very pale, the freckles standing out like scars. 'I don't know how I feel. That's the trouble. I ought to hate her, but I can't. She's lost and lonely. All our lives we've been...close. She's always turned to me in her trouble.'

'And naturally you've been available,' I said, my voice filled with disgust. 'Faithful Adam. Even when she's ignored you for five whole years.'

'Please, Lyn,' Adam said quietly. 'Give me time to sort myself out. I don't want to hurt you.'

I felt very calm, with the numbness which had held me in thrall all day. 'You can't avoid hurting me,' I said. 'But it's my own fault. I've known from the beginning that you loved Jenny. So don't feel guilty about me. If she can make you happy, that's all I ask. *Be* happy. Don't worry about me.'

'You don't understand,' Adam said, his fingers biting into my arms. 'I've changed in these five years. So has Jenny. We don't really know each other any more. I don't know whether I want her now. At the moment I seem to love both of you, for different reasons. I need time to decide.'

'Then I'll save you the trouble. I'm doing what you did once. I'm opting out. You've always loved Jenny and always will. You may not know it, but I do, and so do other people... It's been a very pleasant interlude, Adam. Let's leave it at that.'

'But...' He paused, his face twisting with his inner struggle. 'Jenny still has a career waiting for her in America. She may decide to go back. And if she does, I...'

I twisted away from him, suddenly sick

with loathing. 'Oh, I see! You want to keep your options open! You want to keep me dangling until you find out which way she's going to jump! Well, no, thank you, doctor! I'm not going to play second fiddle. Do you think I'd take my cousin's leavings?'

He had been trying to say something, trying to tell me he had not meant it that way, but I swept all his protests aside.

'You'd better go away! Go away and don't come back!' I ran from him, startling the grey cat, telling myself I hated him.

I didn't, though. I loved him, with such intensity that I thought I must surely break into a million pieces.

* * * *

I did not sleep well that night, but that was because of my emotional state. There was no barking dog to disturb me, no banging doors, and no more panes of glass broken.

What finally woke me was a knocking on the front door and as I struggled out of my lethargy I realised that the sun was high. It was past ten o'clock. I slipped into my dressing-gown, ran my fingers through my hair, and went downstairs.

On the doorstep, wearing slacks and a fringed suede jacket, was my cousin Jenny.

'Oh, heavens!' she exclaimed, looking me up and down. 'Did I get you out of bed? Sorry, Lyn.'

'I didn't realise what time it was,' I said. 'Come in, Jenny.'

She came, and stood surveying the room with a smile. 'It's years since I was in this cottage. Hasn't changed much, has it? Oh...' She glanced at me, violet eyes clouded. 'I was so sorry to hear about your Gran. It must have been a shock.'

'Yes, it was. Can I...offer you some coffee?'

'I'd love some. I really came to ask you to come riding with me. We didn't have much chance to talk yesterday, did we? And it's such a lovely day that I felt like an airing. But Martin's too busy to come, and Melly, as you know, doesn't like to ride.' She perched on the arm of the settee, laughing. 'Guy wanted to escort me, but I couldn't very well let him. Not after being warned off.'

'Warned off by whom?'

'By Melly, of course. Honestly, Lyn, isn't

that girl impossible? She came into my room last night for a chat and eventually confessed, in tears, that she was in love. And when she told me who it was I didn't know whether to laugh or cry.'

'It isn't funny,' I said. 'Melly is so easily hurt.'

'I know that. But—Guy? He won't look twice at her. But she does get these crushes. When I last saw her, she swore she was madly in love with Cliff Richard. That was comparatively harmless, but this... I can only feel sorry for Guy. Melly's the clinging type. Anyway, I'm taking the hint and keeping away from him, though it's not easy. He's a delectable man, isn't he?'

'Yes, I suppose he is quite attractive.'

My cousin laughed. Her laughter, like everything else about her, was beautiful, clear and bell-like. 'Oh, come on, Lyn. You're female, too. Admit it, Guy is a dream. He ought to be in movies. With his looks, he... No, I mustn't keep you talking. You go and get dressed and I'll put the kettle on.'

* * * *

Martin had two sturdy ponies saddled and waiting for us.

'Don't get lost,' he called after us as we rode away.

Jenny shot me a sidelong look from under the brim of the stetson hat she had put on.

'Martin hasn't changed much, has he?' she said. 'Still the arrogant, strutting gamecock. But short men are often like that—compensating for their deficiencies... I suppose you've heard about the plans for the hotel?'

'Yes, I've heard.'

'It's about time something was done. The Mount's like a barn. I always felt we were rattling around in it.'

'Is that why you left?' I asked.

'Partly. And partly the dreary sameness of everything. Hathercombe is so restricting. That's why I'm glad of a chance to talk to *you*. You aren't infected with petty insularity... By the way, I was dreadfully sorry to hear about your parents. Air crash, wasn't it?'

'Yes. They were on their way home from a holiday in Italy. The plane hit some trees as it was taking off.'

'How awful. And how's Bob?'

'Very well. Working in the Middle East at the moment. He was here for Gran's funeral, but he couldn't stay.'

We rode on slowly, swapping news and ideas, until we reached the headland of Morte Point, from where there was a marvellous view of the bay and the three-mile-long beach of Woolacombe Sands. I urged my pony to the edge of the cliff, looking down at the breakers foaming round the base, and turned to say something to Jenny, only to find that she had backed away and was sitting tensely, one hand to her throat, her face white.

'Jenny!' I kicked my heels and turned the pony. 'Jenny, what...oh, I'm sorry. It's the height, isn't it? I'd forgotten. Let's go back. If we cross the road we can get back to Hathercombe through the woods.'

Jenny was silent until we had left the cliff far behind and were approaching the tiny hamlet through which the road ran.

'It makes me so angry with myself,' she said roughly. 'I just can't help it. My head starts to spin and I want to throw myself over the edge. I've never been able to conquer it. You must remember how I could never go down to the cove when we were kids.'

'Yes, I do remember. It was thoughtless of me.' I dismounted to open the gate in the wall and let her go through, closing it behind the two horses.

'Martin never understood,' Jenny said. 'He was always beastly to me. He actually tried to drag me over the cliff one day.'

'I know. I was there. He and Adam fought about it.'

My cousin looked at me, eyes wide with surprise. 'I don't recall your being there. Yes, that was the day I first realised the power a woman has over men. Adam was always my champion after that. It was very flattering—at first. But later on I thought if I didn't escape from him he'd smother me. He was too intense. It frightened me.'

I listened, hoping that she would go on and tell me how she felt now about Adam, but Jenny simply sighed and said, 'Ah, innocent youth! How glad I am to be grown-up. Adolescence is terrible, isn't it? I didn't really know what I wanted, but I wanted it desperately.'

'And have you ever found it?' I asked.

Jenny turned to give me an enigmatic smile, the wide-brimmed hat pulled low over her eyes. 'I know what I want now. And—yes, I believe I've found it.'

We walked the horses single-file down the narrow road until we came to the rutted track which meandered for several miles down through deep woods, skirting Hathercombe village and ending almost opposite the church. Here we turned into the woods, still at a walking pace, and my cousin came up beside me, her face serious.

'Lyn...there's something I must talk to you about. My father...I find it hard to believe that he fell from the cliff path.'

The ponies both stopped and Jenny and I sat staring at each other, Jenny defiant and I astounded to hear her voice my own doubts.

'What...' I choked eventually. 'What makes you say that?'

'Because he was afraid of heights, as I am. You saw what happened to me back there on the headland. My father felt the same. He couldn't go near the cliff edge, much less climb down the path.'

'Have you said this to anyone else?'

'Yes. We had a fine argument last night. And Uncle James had the gall to suggest that Dad killed himself. I was told a lot of rubbish about cancelled builders and disconnected phones... Do you know about that?'

'Yes. And if it's any consolation, Jenny, I feel the same as you do. But when I suggested it they shouted me down.'

'They did me, too. Even Adam pooh-poohed it. He kept going on about the evidence... Eventually I shut up. But I did gather that you'd had similar thoughts. That's why I wanted to talk to you. Then I thought maybe you'd scoff as well..I might be wrong. I'd like to be *proved* wrong. But I just have this feeling... Of course, they say it doesn't matter. They say no matter what happened my father is still dead... Can we sit somewhere and talk about it?'

We found a log which was fairly dry and tethered the ponies to a tree. I sat on the log, while Jenny stood with one foot on it, leaning on her knee.

'Go ahead,' she instructed. 'Tell me.'

'There's little enough to tell. You've heard all their arguments. Your father *was* depressed, I'm not denying that. And I suppose I should tell you another thing—which they probably don't know... A few days before he died, your father gave me his collection of family papers.

That might be construed as preparation for...going away, but I don't think it was. Incidentally, I suppose the papers rightly belong to you now. If you want them...'

'I don't. You're welcome to them... It does sound conclusive, doesn't it? Maybe they're right, after all.'

'Except that your father had this phobia about heights.'

'If he was depressed enough, he might have gone to the cliff on purpose. That's what Uncle James said.'

'But he had a very good reason for staying alive,' I told her, 'which only he and I and Adam know about.'

The dark blue eyes sparked with interest as she sat down beside me.

I asked, 'You know your father's theory about a tunnel?... Well, by a series of circumstances I found out where one end is—in the house. I told your father about it and he was very excited. But since it's in Aunt Maude's room, he had to wait for the right moment... You know how he felt about the Mount. Would he have tried to...to kill himself, before he had explored those stairs?'

'Stairs?'

I told the tale again, of Aunt Maude's

agitation that night and of how she had revealed the secret stairs to me.

'Did you say Adam knows about this? If he...' She broke off, suddenly remembering something, and turned to me to say in an awed voice, 'Oh, Lyn! That's what she meant! Why didn't I... Oh, God!'

'What? What?' I demanded. 'Jenny, tell me.'

She grasped my wrist. 'Listen. This morning I went in to see Aunt Maude after breakfast and she was asking for my father. She kept saying his name, over and over, and asking where he was. I told her he was quite safe...well, that's true, isn't it? Nothing else can ever harm him. But she said, "He went down the stairs and hasn't come back. Where is he, Sonja?"—she always calls me Sonja. I managed to calm her by telling her that I knew where he was and he was perfectly safe. And I thought no more about it. I mean, "the stairs" meant nothing to me then... Lyn, don't you see?'

I saw, all right. Uncle Jonathon had gone to explore the stairs with Aunt Maude's knowledge. He had gone down into the musty darkness I remembered so well and somehow had ended up in the sea.

'We've *got* to look at those stairs,' Jenny said, leaping to her feet. 'One of us can go down while the other stays with Aunt Maude.'

The surprised ponies were kicked into a gallop and we flew through the sunny woods, kicking up clods of earth and sending dead leaves spinning. But our mounts weren't racehorses and soon could be prodded into nothing more than a swift trot, seeming, to our impatient minds, to be crawling.

I saw the road ahead, the shape of the church through the trees, then Jenny reined in her pony and sat with her head cocked.

'Listen!'

Then I heard it, too. A human voice moaning in pain and anguish.

'It's in those bushes,' I said, jumping from the saddle with my cousin behind me. We pushed through the tangle of bushes and stopped in horror at what we saw.

A coloured man lay there—Indian or Pakistani—dressed in crumpled trousers and shirt, an ill-fitting jacket and leather sandals. But what really concerned us was the pallid, bluish tinge of his skin, gleaming with sweat.

He was obviously in great pain. His lank black hair hung down over dark eyes filled with agony and terror and I could hear the hoarse effort of his lungs with every laborious breath.

'What is it?' Jenny asked in a breathless voice.

'I don't know, but it looks serious. You'd better go and telephone a doctor.'

'Better than that. I'll go straight to Adam's house.'

I was left alone in the bird-filled woods, with the wretched man who, I soon discovered, spoke not a word of English. Trying to make him understand that I only wanted to help, I left him and raced across to the cottage, where I filled an empty squash bottle with water and took it back. The man was desperately attempting to crawl away from the place where we found him, but he was much too weak. I had to hold his hand steady before he could drink.

I heard a car screech to a stop on the road and someone brushing hastily past the trees. Then Adam was there, taking in the situation with one horrified glance.

'He's terribly ill,' I said.

'I can see that.' His voice was impersonal,

professional. 'I've sent for an ambulance. Hold him still, Lyn. Does he understand anything?'

'He doesn't seem to.'

He examined the man briskly, putting a stethoscope to the heaving chest and finally injecting penicillin into one scrawny arm.

'What's wrong with him?' I asked.

'Pneumonia,' Adam replied, sitting back on his heels to regard me gravely. 'He's in a very bad way. I'm afraid we may be too late to save him.'

CHAPTER TEN

The following morning, the story was given a quarter-column on the front page of my Sunday newspaper. It said that the man had died shortly after arriving at hospital. His name was not known, but police suspected him of being an illegal immigrant and were anxious to contact anyone who might know him.

The incident was puzzling, but it appeared that my personal involvement with it was over. It didn't occur to me that an unfortunate stranger, dying alone in an alien land, could have a closer connection with the problems which beset me.

⋆ ⋆ ⋆ ⋆

It was Easter Sunday and the weather had risen to the occasion. The only clouds in the blue sky were small fluffy ones, blindingly white and harmless. The road was busy with cars full of families out for the day with their picnic baskets and hopeful bathing suits. I wondered what Adam was doing. Was he out somewhere with Jenny?

I got the shears out and began to attack the front lawn, cutting the grass to a more manageable length, and while I was thus employed, venting my feelings on the defenceless grass, Martin appeared behind the hedge.

'You ought not to be doing that,' he said in the hard tone of the overbearing male.

'Why not?' I demanded, sitting back on my heels and brushing the hair from my eyes. 'I may be a woman, but I'm perfectly capable of...'

'I didn't mean that,' Martin said. 'Haven't you got a mower?'

'There's one in the shed, but it's too heavy for me to use. I don't know what Gran used to do.'

'I think Mr Tregannon did it for her.' He walked to the gate, came through it and marched determinedly down the path. 'I'll see if the mower's serviceable.'

A few minutes later, I heard the machine trundling down by the side of the house.

'It only needed a bit of oil,' Martin told me. 'Move out of the way and let me have a go.'

He cut one long strip of grass and turned to grin at me as he leaned on the mower handle.

'See how easy it is? A little masculine know-how...'

'The mower's still too heavy for me,' I said. 'I don't suppose you'd care to finish the job now you've started?'

'Might as well. I thought I'd come and keep you company for a while. The others have gone out picnicking.'

'All of them?' I asked.

Martin laughed softly and said with some amusement. 'Only the younger generation. I'm not sure how it came about—who asked whom or whatever, but all three of them were going. And then Jenny suggested asking Adam along, so they all went off in Adam's car. I suspect that Guy asked Jenny but she wouldn't go without Melly. My sister has got one hell of a crush on our revered step-brother.'

'Yes, I know that. Poor Melly.'

'Poor Guy! Imagine what it must be like to have a lump of lard like Melly fussing around you.'

'Melly's a very sweet girl,' I said angrily. 'Kind and loving and...'

'And fat and spotty,' Martin supplied, then held up his hands in surrender. 'Don't let's fight, Lyn. I came to cheer you up, not to argue about Melly.' Hazel eyes met mine, suddenly full of sympathy. 'I know how you must be feeling,' he said quietly. 'You and Adam were doing fine until that spoiled bitch showed up. He's a fool to let her use him. I know which one *I'd* prefer, if I had a choice.'

'Flattery from you?' I said in astonishment, trying to conceal the turmoil he had started inside me. I hadn't needed reminding of how jealous I was of Jenny.

'I said the same thing to Adam,' Martin told me.

'Did you?' I turned away, hiding my distress. 'And what did he say?'

'Nothing.' He sounded as if he were laughing. 'I think he was tempted to belt me one, but he controlled himself. He never could accept the truth about Jenny.'

'I think I'll make some tea,' I said, and fled into the cottage.

* * * *

When I returned, with two cups on a tray, Martin was in argument with a group of teenage boys who were outside on the pavement. Two of them wore jeans with braces showing over T-shirts, and their hair was cropped short. The other three were more conventionally dressed, but they all had the same defiant expression.

'These lads have been roaming round our grounds,' Martin said in an aggrieved tone.

'Yeah,' said one of the 'skinheads', 'so sue us. We done no harm. And it don't say Private nor nuffink. We was only takin' a walk.'

The other lads nodded agreement, swaggering in front of my irate cousin.

'They're right,' I said. 'There's nothing you can do about it, Martin.'

'Hey, lady,' one of the boys said, a dark, intelligent looking boy with wickedly-smiling eyes. 'Is he your boy-friend?'

The others sniggered. Martin said loudly, 'No, I'm not. Why don't you louts clear off?'

They made no move to leave. The dark one was watching me, as if amused by some secret joke.

'How's the other one making out, then?' he asked. 'The one with the red Jag? Did you collapse in his arms like he planned?'

The skinhead nudged him and said, 'Watch it, Hal.'

The dark one shrugged. 'It won't make no difference. After all, we was paid to do it. If she sets the fuzz on us we'll cough the lot and get her boy-friend in shtook. Or maybe we'll come back some time and smash *all* the windows.'

While I was struggling to understand the implications of all this, Martin glanced at me with a frown before returning his attention to the youths.

'Let's get this straight,' he said. 'You were paid to break this young lady's windows—by a man with a red Jaguar?'

'Sure.' The boy with the malicious gleam in his eyes was supremely confident, carelessly confessing to vandalism. 'We met him one night, down the road there. He gave us a quid to do something to frighten this bird he fancied, so that he could arrive on the doorstep and play the shining knight.'

I remembered that night—how Guy had come immediately after the smashing of the first window. But his plans had gone awry because Adam had been with me.

'Guy has a peculiar way of showing his devotion,' Martin said darkly, and swung back to the boys. 'I shall remember you—all of you. And if I see you round this way again there'll be trouble. There are four windows to pay for, not to mention...'

'Four?' said the smallest of the boys, turning pale. 'No, not four. We only chucked one brick. It couldn't've...'

The dark one thrust him aside and came to stand close to the hedge, eyes narrowed. 'What are you trying to do, mister?' he demanded in a threatening voice. 'We told the truth, didn't we? Thought the lady might like to know. But it was once, see? Only once. One brick. One window. So don't you try to stick us with any more. You say anything, we'll deny the lot. And then we'll come and get you!'

'Try me!' Martin returned, chin thrust out. 'You bloody yobs think you can get away with anything.'

They stood where they were, measuring him, four of them waiting for a word from the dark one. The air felt heavy with menace. Martin was sturdy, but there were five of those boys and though they were much younger than my cousin they all looked tough, except for the smallest one, who was struggling not to let his apprehension show.

But we were there in the open, with cars going by at irregular intervals. The dark boy, the leader of the gang, clearly considered the moment unpropitious.

He thrust up two fingers in an obscene manner, spat a couple of dirty words, and turned to saunter away, saying something that made the others laugh loudly.

'Don't!' I gasped as Martin started towards the gate and he stopped and turned towards me, flinging his arms up helplessly.

'What was I supposed to do?' he demanded. 'Let them stand there and talk to us like that? Damn it all, Lyn, they smashed your windows.'

'They smashed one. The others...that

was different. It wasn't boys who made that dog bark or banged on my door at two in the morning.'

'Then who was it? You don't think... Guy? Maybe he wanted you up at the Mount, where he could put pressure on you. Did he?'

I shook my head, puzzled by it all. 'After that night...when the first window was broken...he hasn't taken any notice of me. I don't understand it, Martin. Why should he want to frighten me?'

'Damaged pride, I expect. Do you want me to ask him about it?' He flexed his shoulders and arms, belligerent again, imagining what he would do to Guy.

I appreciated his protective instinct, but didn't want to be the cause of trouble. 'No. Don't bother. We can't prove anything. I'll pour some more tea. This must be cold by now.'

Going back into the cottage, I wondered again about Guy's motives. Adam had said something about someone trying to frighten me away but I had discounted it, until now. There seemed no rhyme or reason to it. But... I paused, the teapot poised in my hand, and stared out of the window to where Martin was mowing the lawn... What had happened to Adam here in this cottage? Was it possible that he had not injured himself on that low beam? I had found some blood there. Only a smear, but... I shook myself angrily. I was imagining things again, getting neurotic. There was nothing wrong here at Smugglers' Cottage. There couldn't be.

Smugglers' Cottage. It was called that because of the cellar hidden under the flagstones of the kitchen. As a child, I remember I was shown the pivoted stone and the dank darkness beneath. But the cellar had been blocked off for ever when my father had the cottage renovated for Gran. There was now a concrete floor covered by modern tiles.

I remembered Uncle Jonathon and the letter which was now in my possession. Smugglers had come to the cove and disappeared right under the noses of the customs men waiting on the cliff. And those stairs at Hathercombe Mount... So many disconnected pieces. Mysteries in the past and in the present. Gran and Smokey. Uncle Jonathon...

Martin put his head round the back door, startling me.

'You were miles away,' he laughed. 'Is that tea ready yet? I'm thirsty after all my hard work.' He took the cup from me, drained it, and wiped his mouth inelegantly on the back of his hand. 'Well, I must be going. Got to see the pony-trekkers safely home. I've put the mower away.'

'Thanks, Martin. It was very kind of you to...'

He shrugged off my gratitude and went away with a negligent wave of his hand.

* * * *

Having eaten the little food I felt like, I built a small fire and sat by the window watching the procession of cars returning from the country or the beach. Other people, I thought, had been out enjoying themselves all day while I fought my depression. Adam and Jenny, Melly and Guy. Laughing and eating their picnic lunch. My imagination supplied vivid details of what those two young couples had been doing and I felt more and more sorry for myself. Eventually, giving in to loneliness and self-pity, I put my head down on my arm and let the tears come.

The gate clicked. Lifting my head I saw Adam coming down the path. He saw me, too, so it was no use my pretending not to be in. I left my seat and hurriedly dried my face before opening the door. I didn't look at Adam, but stood with my face averted.

'I'd like to talk to you,' he said in a toneless voice. 'May I come in?'

'I can't prevent you,' I replied, moving back to the window and staring out of it, blinking hard and wondering how long it would take for my face to get rid of the traces of tears.

'You only have to say I'm not welcome,' Adam said flatly. 'I wanted to talk to you, but if you'd rather not see me, I...'

I slumped into a chair, one hand to my aching head. 'You're here. Don't go on about it. I'm in no mood.'

'I can see that,' he said more quietly. 'Are you feeling depressed?'

Of all the stupid questions! My voice dripped sarcasm as I replied, 'What on earth have I got to be depressed about? Everything's fine, isn't it... Oh, take no notice. I'm just feeling sorry for myself.'

The settee creaked as he sat down on it and there was a long silence, so that I turned to look at Adam and found him frowning towards the fire. I felt like screaming at him. I didn't want him here. Hadn't he just spent the day with Jenny, probably come to me straight from her arms, with her kisses still warm on his face?

'What is it you want?' It ought to have been a cry, but it came out as a hoarse whisper.

Adam looked round slowly. It was clear from his expression that he had something he wanted to say but didn't know how to phrase it and was perhaps considering the wisdom of saying anything at all while I was in my present state.

'I saw Jenny today,' he said.

'You amaze me,' I replied with bitter irony, wanting to hit out and hurt him as I had been hurt.

Adam looked wretched, his eyes full of unhappiness and indecision. 'I only wanted to warn you. This crazy notion about Jonathon... You shouldn't have encouraged her. The best thing you can both do is forget it. Jonathon's dead and nothing will bring him back. Jenny had accepted that until she talked to you. And now she's got some foolish idea about the secret stairs.'

'Is it so foolish?'

'I think so. You can't rely on something Miss Maude said.'

'We shan't know about that until we've explored the stairs.'

Adam's mouth set in hard lines and when he spoke his voice was grim. 'I will not have Miss Maude disturbed and upset just to satisfy your curiosity. Is that quite clear?'

'Perfectly. I assume you said the same to Jenny?'

'I did. And she agreed, eventually. She wasn't any more pleased about it than you are. She actually asked *me* to sit with Miss Maude while she investigated the stairs. But I want nothing to do with it. Best all round if the matter is allowed to rest. Do I have your word?'

I bit my lip, unable to meet his eyes. 'I promise not to disturb Aunt Maude, but that's all. I can't stop thinking about it. And I can't believe Uncle Jonathon fell off the cliff.'

'Not even deliberately?' Adam said harshly.

I looked at him, startled and angry. 'No. Especially not that. Not when he was on the verge of...'

'Lyn!' His voice cut across mine like a

whiplash. 'Use your head. I didn't want to have to say this but... Maybe Jonathon did explore those stairs. And found nothing. The way closed off. The tunnel caved in. It would destroy his last hope, his last reason for living.'

The fire spat into the silence and outside a young couple walking by burst into laughter.

'You can't believe that!' I breathed, horrified. 'But if it's true... Don't you want to know?'

Adam shook his head hard, dislodging a lock of chestnut hair which fell across his forehead. 'I'd rather believe it was an accident. Much rather. And Jenny needn't ever suspect that...'

'Jenny!' I leapt to my feet, furious. 'Jenny, Jenny, Jenny! I don't give a damn about Jenny. What did she ever do for her father except make him miserable? If he killed himself, she ought to know. She contributed to it! What's so special about her that she must be pampered and shielded? I'll bet she's a damn sight tougher than she looks. How on earth do you suppose she's managed out in the big world all this time without your protective care?'

Adam was looking at me as if I had hit him, but instead of feeling victorious I was suddenly deflated, the wild mixture of anger and jealousy leaving me with a rush like the air from a pricked balloon. I was behaving like a hoyden. The proverbial woman scorned. I didn't want to hurt him. I loved him.

Unable to face him for a moment longer, I turned and made a mad rush for the stairs. And as I reached my room I heard the front door open and close with horrible finality. Adam had gone.

I lay on my bed, thumping the pillow, ugly sounds tearing from my throat, my eyes scalding. Adam was gone, gone, gone, and this time he wouldn't come back.

* * * *

A hand came on my shoulder and I jerked round to stare in disbelief at Adam, standing beside the bed with a glass of water in one hand and two tablets on the palm of the other. I stared stupidly at him, my head pounding.

'These will make you feel better,' he said. 'Take them.'

I sat up, silently accepting the tablets

and the water. Not looking at Adam, I gulped them down and returned the glass, then lay down with my back towards him, expecting him to leave me. I heard him put the glass down on the pink-painted chest of drawers and then there was no sound but my own uneven breathing.

I felt the bed give as he sat down beside me, and he said in a strange, quiet voice, 'Tranquillisers are a pretty lousy present. I should have brought you flowers or chocolates but the shops were all closed.'

'Why should you bring me anything?' I choked.

'It's usual, isn't it, when a man comes to ask forgiveness?' His hand came again onto my shoulder, insistent this time. 'Please, Lyn, look at me.'

I rolled onto my back, knowing that my eyes were swollen, my face blotchy, still unable to believe that he meant what I thought he meant. Adam's fingers smoothed my hair as he struggled for words that wouldn't come until he gave up trying to communicate by speech. He bent over me swiftly, his lips meeting mine, his upper body pinning me to the bed, saying things more eloquently than any words. For a moment I was too dazed to do anything, then the heady joy surged up in me and I locked my arms about his neck, returning his kiss with an equal passion that drove all else from my mind.

His lips roamed over my face, traced my jawline, my throat, and rested there, his breath coming warm against my skin. I could feel him shaking.

'Let me go,' he said breathlessly. 'Darling girl, for both our sakes...'

I unclasped my arms, let them fall, and Adam raised himself up, braced with his hands either side of me, hanging there above me with the hunger deep in his eyes.

'I was wrong,' he said in a gruff voice. 'All I feel for Jenny is pity, and the kind of affection you do feel for an old friend. But not love. Not any more. That's all for you now.'

'Why didn't you tell me?' I breathed.

'I couldn't. You'd sent me away. You might have meant it.'

'Oh...Adam!' I got out, torn between laughter and tears.

Adam smiled ruefully. 'I know. I'm a fool. But I hurt you terribly and... You misunderstood me, Lyn. I tried to explain but you wouldn't listen. I thought that if Jenny decided to go back to America it would finally destroy what I felt for her. But it isn't so. It doesn't make any difference whether she stays or goes. You're all that matters to me. A day with Jenny has made that clear. I don't understand how I could have doubted for a minute that you were the one. Forgive me, Lyn.'

Unable to speak, I raised my hands to his face and he bent over me again, only our lips touching, in an endless kiss that made my whole being vibrate with longing.

'I'll make some coffee,' he said softly. 'You wash your face and then come down.'

I nodded wordlessly, too full to speak, and followed him from the bedroom. From the landing I saw him pause at the beam across the stairs, running his fingers along it thoughtfully.

'I suppose,' he said slowly, 'I might have come downstairs in a hurry and half ducked...like this, not quite far enough.' His fingers moved through his hair, where the blood had been. 'Possible. Where did you find the blood?'

'Right there, in the middle. Only...' I paused uncertainly. 'I'm not sure now,

Adam. You don't suppose someone could have dabbed blood on the beam to make it look like...'

He glanced up at me, eyes narrowed. 'Someone? What do you mean?'

'I don't really know. We'll talk about it in a minute.'

I went into the small bathroom and bathed my face with cold water. A little make-up disguised the damage caused by tears and I changed my crumpled clothes for a pretty dress.

Adam was in the kitchen, bending down by the open door, his hand held out towards the conservatory, where the grey cat stood eyeing him cautiously, her eyes gleaming gold in the shaft of light from the kitchen.

'Poor thing,' I said. 'I don't know what chance her kittens will stand when they're born. I keep leaving bits out for her, but...'

Adam, I realised, wasn't listening. He remained on his haunches, hand still out, as if turned to stone.

'Adam?' I queried.

'Just a minute, darling,' he said briskly. 'I've just...' He stood up, very slowly, and just as slowly stepped through the door, half turned, while I watched in surprise.

'That morning,' he said. 'When you came and found me out cold. How did you get in?'

'This door was unlocked. Adam, what...'

His eyes met mine and the expression in them was not pleasant. 'I've remembered what really happened. I was asleep on the settee when something woke me. An engine, I think, on the Mount driveway. I thought nothing of it and was going back to sleep when I heard another noise—like a sharp bang on metal. It was somewhere out the back here. I came into the kitchen, put the light on, unlocked the door, stepped out... There was someone in here, in the conservatory, waiting in that corner. And as I started to turn, he hit me.'

Words failed me. I stood and stared in horrified silence.

'The question is,' Adam said, 'why? Have you got anything valuable in the cottage?'

I shook my head, swallowing to stop the dryness in my throat. 'Nothing. And there's nothing missing.'

He came back into the kitchen, closed the door and leaned on it. 'Are you sure that was blood on the beam?'

'Positive. And when I found it I

was certain that... Adam, whoever it was—he couldn't have known you wouldn't remember.'

'No, that's true. But he confused the issue nicely, didn't he? Got me to the bottom of the stairs, smeared some of my blood on the beam. Doesn't something occur to you, Lyn?'

'No,' I said dazedly. 'What?'

'Whoever it was—whoever hit me, and for whatever reason—it must have been someone who knew the cottage, knew about that low beam. It was probably someone we both know.'

* * * *

He put some more coal on the fire and we sat by it as we had done a good many times, with the coffee pot and cups in front of us.

'And now,' Adam said, drawing me into the circle of his arm, 'you can tell me what made you suspicious.'

'Something you said actually—about my poltergeist being a human who wanted to scare me away from here. If that was true, then it worked, except that you were here instead of me, and you didn't stay cowering behind locked doors the way I did. You went out. Oh, Adam, what is it all about? Why should Guy do such...'

'Guy?' he said sharply, looking down into my face.

'I can't think who else it could be,' I sighed. 'You see, Guy paid some boys to break a window...yes, paid. They were outside earlier and told us—Martin was here at the time. You do remember that you saw them running away and then Guy came immediately after...'

'Yes, I remember that. But these boys...did Guy tell them his reasons?'

'He told them he fancied me and wanted to come to console me after my fright. But I'm not so sure that was true. I mean...having established it as vandalism, everybody would discount the later happenings... Everybody did,' I added flatly. 'But it doesn't make sense. What's been going on here? First Gran and Smokey; then all those disturbances; then you...' I put a hand to my whirling head. 'I can't seem to think straight.'

'You've forgotten something,' Adam said gravely. 'I admit there's no real connection, but...that man you found. Apparently an illegal immigrant. And he can't have been in this country long.'

'I'm afraid I don't follow you.'

Adam pulled me closer, pressing my head into the hollow of his shoulder. 'Those tablets are making you sleepy. I'll let you rest in a minute... But don't you see? Not so very far from here there is a secluded cove, perfect for the landing of illicit goods—including human beings. And to get away from that cove, where do they have to come?'

I thought about it, my brain working sluggishly. 'Up the cliff, past the Mount, down the...' I looked up at him. 'The driveway?'

'Exactly,' Adam said. 'That's an interesting thought, isn't it? Especially when you remember that this cottage is the only inhabited place anywhere near the drive.'

CHAPTER 11

Overnight, the weather changed. A cold front swept in from the Atlantic, bringing a layer of cloud which, when I woke, was glowing a sullen red in the East. It felt more like autumn than spring and there was a misty rain hanging in the air.

It was cold in the cottage so I pulled on some slacks, a blouse and a thick sweater, going down to make a fire before I did anything else. The grey cat was waiting for me outside, but it was not until I had put out her milk that I noticed the change in her. Her body was thin, though not so thin as when I had first seen her. The swelling of pregnancy had gone. She must have given birth during the night.

'Where are they?' I asked. 'Where are your kittens?'

The cat continued lapping, not nearly so nervous of me as she had been. I wondered how many kittens she had produced, and how they would survive in the wild, but doubted that I would ever know the answer.

As soon as the milk was gone the cat sat down to wash herself, completely at home, and as I watched her I saw Jenny coming hurriedly down the road from the Mount, wearing a short, hooded cloak and scarlet slacks. She waved to me and called, 'Hi, Lyn, I'm coming to see you. Get the coffee on.'

What now? I wondered, feeling suddenly

edgy. She hadn't sounded annoyed with me, but perhaps she didn't realise that Adam had made his choice. Or was she coming to talk some more about Uncle Jonathon?

She knocked on the front door and came in, throwing back the hood and shaking out her pale hair.

'It's freezing!' she announced. 'Honestly, coming straight from Texas to the vagaries of an English spring... It's not very warm in here, either.'

'I've only just lit the fire,' I replied. 'Come and sit down.'

I took a seat by the window and let Jenny have the chair pulled up to the hearth. She unhooked her cloak and flung it back, holding her hands out to the blaze.

'I thought you'd like to know,' she said. 'We investigated those stairs. It was a waste of time. They go nowhere. Aunt Maude must have been imagining things. I should never have let you talk me into it.'

'I think that's unfair,' I replied. 'It was you who...'

'Oh yes, well, whether or not,' she interrupted swiftly. 'As I wasn't here when the accident happened I was naturally anxious to find out as much as I could. But that's always been your trouble—too much imagination. I mean to say—thinking you were being haunted.' She looked over her shoulder at me. 'Have you thought about seeing a psychiatrist? They can do wonders, these days... Oh, don't look so shocked, Lyn. I'm only thinking of you. After everything you've been through...'

'There's nothing wrong with me,' I said levelly, containing my annoyance with difficulty. 'You came to tell me about the secret stairs, and you said "we" investigated them. Who did you tell?'

'Oh, God, I might have known you'd pounce on that.' She stood up, rubbing her arms, tall and slender in the black sweater and bright slacks. 'I don't see much point in keeping it a deathly secret. I tried. I asked Adam to help, but he's got so stuffy about Aunt Maude. Didn't want to "disturb" the old girl—as if she ever knows what time it is. So I told Martin and *he* went down last night, while I sat with Aunt Maude. It didn't take him long to find out that there may have been a tunnel once but it's caved in.'

So Adam, I thought, had been right. Most probably Uncle Jonathon had discovered the same thing.

'I take it,' Jenny said sarcastically, 'that you'll allow Martin into the secret. He *is* a member of the family. So I'm convinced that my father had an accident. I expect he was trying to get down to the cove to look for himself. It's the sort of crazy thing he might do... It sounds as though your kettle's boiling.'

I hurried through to the kitchen and made two cups of instant coffee, seething with anger. Jenny had broken two promises—her promise to me about preserving secrecy, which had been her father's wish, and her promise to Adam that she would not bother Aunt Maude.

'Was Aunt Maude upset?' I asked as I handed her the cup.

Jenny shrugged carelessly. 'A bit. She didn't understand what was going on. But she's forgotten all about it this morning.'

'I hope you're right,' I said. 'Adam's not going to be very pleased when he finds out. I thought you promised him you wouldn't...'

'I didn't exactly promise. I just let him think that...' The violet eyes narrowed as they fastened on my face. 'Who told you about that?'

'Adam did. He came last night, to tell me the same thing he told you. He was worried about the effect our explorations might have on Aunt Maude.'

'Oh, really!' Jenny sighed, sinking back into the chair. 'Isn't that typical! As if it was any business of his.'

'He *is* her doctor,' I reminded her. 'And when Adam cares about something, he cares deeply.'

She sipped her coffee slowly, while I returned to my seat by the window.

'I gather I rather stepped on your toes,' she said eventually, looking at me from her eye corners, through a curtain of ash-blonde hair. 'Melly told me. But it isn't my fault if Adam can't get me out of his system. He's always been like that. I must say it's rather nice to know I have a faithful admirer, but I'm sorry that you had to be caught in between.' She sighed heavily, shaking back her hair. 'Poor Adam. It's a pity I have to disappoint him again. I can't bear the thought of settling in Hathercombe—with a doctor of all people. Imagine the ruination to your social life! I haven't had the heart to tell him yet, but I'm more or less engaged to Grant Pearson—he's a Texan. Oil wells and all that. I was staying with his family when the news came. And if I don't get back soon, Grant is threatening to come and get me—he rang me yesterday evening. Luckily Adam had just gone, or I'd have had to tell him there and then. I know he's still hoping. I only hope he doesn't try to propose again. If I can get away before he works up the courage...'

'Adam asked you to marry him?' I broke in, my voice sharper than I intended.

Jenny looked at me in surprise. 'Didn't you know? I suppose you ought to—if you're planning to try to console him. Are you, incidentally?'

'I may do,' I said, content in the knowledge that Adam had made his decision before he knew what Jenny's plans were.

'Well, you can always try,' she said smugly. 'Though I do warn you—he's a one-woman man. He'll die a bachelor. You might be wise not to ask for any more hurt. There are men like that, you know, loving one woman all their lives, whether available or not.'

'And even when she's a self-centred cow,' I said.

My cousin sat up, glaring at me. 'Don't blame me! I'm not responsible for his obsession. I told him I didn't want to settle down. I never asked him to wait.'

'No, I know you didn't. But you let him believe there might be hope. You're good at letting people believe things, Jenny. But you were telling me—about five years ago.'

'Yes!' Her eyes glittered furiously. 'Five years ago, when Adam and I were lovers... You should see your face! Where have you been living lately, in a nunnery?... Yes, it was like that. Not regular, but often enough, and his devotion was flattering. He must have spent nearly all his salary on me. Only it never occurred to me that he took it as a permanent relationship. He assumed that when he'd finished his residency we would get married. Assumed it! Without a word to me. I didn't think he could be so stupid. He knew I wanted to make something of my career, yet you should have heard what he said when I told him I was going to work in America. That was the first time I'd heard anything about marriage. I was absolutely astonished. I thought he was joking.' She laughed, a little uncertainly, and spread her hands. 'What could I do? I'd had no intention of getting married. I mean, he actually expected me to give up my big chance and come back with him and...vegetate. How about that for super-egotism? Never by word or deed had I indicated that I wanted marriage.'

'You slept with him,' I said bitterly.

'So what? Just because you let a man into your bed it doesn't mean you want to spend the rest of your life with him.'

'Doesn't it?'

Irritably, Jenny searched the pocket of her cloak and brought out a pack of American cigarettes and a tiny gold lighter.

'Naturally you wouldn't understand,' she said, blowing out a thin stream of smoke. 'I don't know why I bothered to tell you, except that you might as well know what sort of man Adam is. If he'd had any pride he would have left it at that, but he rang me up just before I left and told me he'd be waiting, if I changed my mind.'

'And you believed that he would,' I said flatly. 'When you saw him again, you took it for granted that he had waited, and you were prepared to use him—until you went away again. Didn't you care what that might do to him?'

Jenny blinked. It was clear that she had never looked at it from Adam's point of view. To her, there was no point of view but her own, and she was supremely confident of her own power.

'Do to him?' she repeated. 'I thought it would make him happy for a short while.'

'My God!' I breathed in utter disbelief. 'The goddess handing out favours to her worshippers.'

Jenny threw her cigarette into the fire, stood up and jerked the cloak round her shoulders. 'I see no point in continuing this conversation. You can do what you like with Adam. I suppose he might settle for second best.'

'Grant Pearson has my sympathy,' I said as she swept to the door.

The red spots on her cheeks made her eyes look unnaturally bright. 'Grant Pearson,' she said through her teeth, '*adores* me. I doubt that you'll ever be able to say the same about any man.' She opened the door, said, 'Goodbye, Lynda,' with finality, and paused as she saw Adam coming in the gate.

'Are you looking for me?' Jenny asked. 'I'm just coming.'

'Just going, you mean,' Adam corrected, smiling through the window at me. 'I've come to see Lyn.'

'About what? Or is this a professional call?'

'Not likely. We have a code of ethics about that sort of thing. I'm not Lyn's doctor.' He came into the cottage and said, 'Am I?' to me.

'Certainly not,' I said.

'Oh,' Jenny said blankly. 'I see. Well...I'll see you later, Adam. You will be coming up to the Mount, won't you?'

'I hadn't planned to,' he replied.

Jenny stared at him for a moment, then looked at me, saying angrily, 'No wonder you're feeling so bloody smug! Well, *you* have *my* sympathy!'

Her footsteps tapped sharply down the path before Adam closed the door, glancing at me enquiringly.

'What was all that about?'

'We've just been having a cosy chat. Girl to girl stuff. All about you, as a matter of fact... Adam, do you realise what you just did?'

'Made things crystal clear to her, I

hope... I'd have been here earlier, but I've just been to the police station.'

'The police!' Instantly I forgot all about Jenny. 'What did they say?'

Smiling ruefully, Adam sat down on the edge of the settee. 'They're going to look into it, so don't be surprised if a horde of them descend on this place. Of course I had to go into long involved explanations about why I hadn't reported it to them before.'

'Did you tell them about Guy?' I asked.

'Some of it. I expect they'll want to hear the whole thing from you, and probably get descriptions of those boys. Do you think you could describe them?'

'I could try, and Martin would help... Would you like some coffee?'

He followed me into the kitchen, bringing Jenny's empty cup with him. Placing it on the draining-board, he said slowly, 'What was Jenny saying about me?'

'Only that you were so crazy about her I didn't stand a chance. I never realised she was quite so conceited.' I had my back to him, putting sugar and coffee into the cups.

'Neither did I,' Adam said. 'Not until

yesterday. For the first time in my life I was able to stand back and look at her objectively. And to think I wasted five years just thinking about her, hoping that some day... I've been a fool, haven't I?'

I turned then, and put my arms tightly around him, hiding my face against his thick sweater. 'Whatever you've been, it doesn't matter to me. As long as you're sure now.'

'I couldn't be more sure,' he said quietly, his hands caressing my hair and shoulders. 'But there's something I've got to tell you, Lyn. Jenny and I were...'

'No,' I lifted my head. 'No, don't tell me. I already know what was between you. Jenny told me. I understand now why you were so badly upset. We've both made mistakes. But not any more. This time, we both know what...'

The sweet firmness of his mouth stopped what I had been going to say, confirming our mutual feelings with an eloquence beyond words.

* * * *

I was pouring hot water into the cups when Adam remarked, 'It looks as though your cat's bringing you an offering.'

Joining him at the window, I saw the grey cat deposit something behind the pile of old newspapers in the corner of the conservatory before bounding out into the garden.

'What was it?' I asked.

'I couldn't see. Maybe a mouse. Shall I have a look?'

He went out, across to the corner, while I stood by the kitchen door, ready to slam it if a mouse darted out. Adam glanced round and held out his hand. 'Come and see.'

I went, cautiously, and saw, there in the sheltered corner, the tiny bedraggled body of a new-born kitten. Its eyes were tightly closed and its little red mouth opened to emit a shrill squeak.

'You appear to have acquired a family,' Adam said with a smile. 'I wonder where she brought it from?'

The rain had stopped as we went out into the garden. The cat was edging sinuously through the fence at the end, carrying another kitten by the scruff of the neck. She paused when she saw us, then darted past and went into the conservatory.

'Looks as though she gave birth in the

wilderness,' Adam said, 'but obviously it isn't considered a proper place for bringing up a family.'

'She always makes for the copse,' I said. 'But the first time I saw her she was down at the cove. Remember those scattered nests in the cave?'

By the time the cat returned, Adam and I were at the bottom of the garden. We watched her leap away through the bushes and disappear between two boulders on a slope where a trailing growth of branches covered the ground. To my surprise, Adam reached up to the branch of an apple tree and swung himself over the fence, dropping down the other side.

'Whatever are you doing?' I asked.

'Curiosity,' Adam said. 'And a crazy idea I just had. You wait there.'

He brushed through the wet grass and clinging brambles, stepping aside as the cat came past him with a third kitten. When she was safely on her way, Adam ducked below the branches of a hawthorn tree and pushed on, until he reached the two boulders. I saw him bend to study the ground, then lift the fresh green branches which obscured the gap between the rocks.

Again the cat returned, coming past me as though I weren't there, and Adam retreated to let her back into her hiding place.

'Have you got a torch?' he called.

'Yes, but...what is it?'

'You can see for yourself in a minute. But bring that torch.'

On my way, I had a look at the three tiny kittens, and as I left the cottage with Gran's heavy-duty rubber torch the cat brought a fourth of her offspring. Adam took the torch and helped me over the fence, leading me by the hand through the soaking undergrowth to the two pale boulders and the waterfall of branches.

'Look at that.' He pointed to a patch of bare earth under one of the rocks, where there was a clearly defined human shoe print. 'And these branches—some of them are split across. And behind you—see where the grasses are bent down, where someone has walked through them? What do you make of it?'

'How deep is that hole?' I asked sharply, as Adam's 'crazy idea' took shape in my own mind.

'That,' he said, 'is what I should like

to know. Hang on, here comes your fifth baby.'

The cat emerged from the hole between the two boulders, bearing yet another kitten in her mouth.

'That sounds like the lot,' Adam said. 'I could hear them crying before.'

He shone the torch into the opening, revealing a steeply-sloping tunnel about ten feet long. At the bottom there was a scattering of tiny bones—the remains of the cat's meals. Beyond, the torchlight led away into darkness.

Adam looked at me, his freckled face alive with excitement. 'I'm going down. You stay here. I may need a hand to get out.'

He let himself down, feet first, into the hole. There was a pattering of earth and Adam slid from sight. I heard him exclaim sharply as he fetched up with a thud.

'Adam!' I called anxiously.

His voice came to me hollowly. 'I'm all right. God, it stinks in here...! Lyn, it does go on. I can't see how far...'

'Wait for me!' I called, crawling backwards into the tunnel.

I managed to go down more slowly, digging my toes in as the daylight faded to a big round patch above me. Adam was right about the stench. It was all dampness, dirt and cats. Disgusting.

'We shall both need a bath,' he said dolefully. 'Don't stand up too suddenly. It's not very high.'

The torchlight swung round, showing me the tunnel which led off downwards through the rock. The walls and ceiling glistened with water, which lay in pools on the uneven floor.

'Jonathon was right, after all,' Adam said in a hushed voice. 'There's a through-draught from somewhere. Mind your head as we go.'

He led the way, following the torchlight, his free hand clasped tightly around mine. After a few yards he was able to walk almost upright. The tunnel appeared to level out. It stretched ahead of us, rough-hewn from the living rock.

'You know where it's heading,' Adam said. 'Towards the cove... You're shivering. Do you want to go back?'

'Not on your life!' I muttered. 'Not till I know where this comes out.'

We went on, our footsteps echoing down the tunnel. It was very cold and water dripped on us from the ceiling. There was a musical plinking as some of the drops found the puddles on the floor. A different world. Where smugglers had once walked.

'Ssh!' Adam stopped so abruptly that I bumped into him and stayed there, glad of his warmth, as we both listened intently.

It came again, the clink of rock against rock, bouncing along the tunnel to reach our ears. And then there was the sharp, brittle sound of several rocks rolling.

'What is it?' I breathed.

'It doesn't sound like a cave-in,' Adam whispered. 'Wait here while I...'

'In the dark? Not likely.'

'Well, at least stay behind me. We don't know...'

He was cut off by a voice which boomed at us from the darkness ahead.

'Who's there? Who is that?'

* * * *

The words reverberated in the confined space, but no amount of distortion could disguise that familiar voice.

'It's Martin!' I exclaimed.

'Lyn?' said my cousin's disembodied

voice. 'Is that you, Lynda? Who's with you?'

'Adam Taylor,' Adam replied. 'Where are you, Martin?'

Martin appeared at the edge of our torchlight, his own torch deflected to the floor. He was wearing a russet sweater and faded jeans, with a pair of white plimsolls.

'Good grief!' he exclaimed. 'You gave me the fright of my life. Where on earth did you come from?'

'We might ask you the same,' Adam said mildly.

'I came down the secret stairs,' my cousin explained. 'You did know about them, I gather?'

'We did. But who told you?'

'Jenny did. She talked me into coming down and...where does this tunnel go?'

'It comes out behind Smugglers' Cottage,' Adam said. 'And who is sitting with Miss Maude? If you've upset her...'

'Oh, no, she's all right. Well...so now we know where the famous tunnel is. There's a T-junction back here. It leads to the cave.'

Adam moved forward, taking me with him. 'Can you get out into the cave?'

'No. It's blocked off.'

'Are you sure?' Adam asked.

Martin flung an arm up over his eyes. 'Keep the light down, can't you? You're blinding me.'

Behind him, now that we were nearer, I could see the blank wall at the end of the tunnel, with two openings to left and right. But why had Martin told Jenny the stairs were blocked? And why had he come back to the tunnel? I wished that I had told Adam that Martin had already explored the stairs, but I couldn't tell him now. I was waiting for Martin to explain himself.

'There *has* to be a way out,' Adam said, half to himself. 'I'm sure this tunnel's being used. It's the only thing that would explain all that's happened.'

Martin's face looked strange in the combined light of both torches, lit from beneath, so that the shadows were all in the wrong places.

'Being used?' he repeated. 'For what?'

'I'm not sure. That's what I want to find out.'

'You don't think...' Martin began, and licked his lips. 'Is that why Guy was so anxious to have Lynda away from the cottage?'

'It appears to be. Move out of the way, Martin. We want to...'

It was time, I decided, that I spoke up and did so, cutting across what Adam was saying. 'Why did you tell Jenny the way was blocked?'

Martin's face went blank and I saw beads of sweat sparkle on his forehead. 'Why... Have you seen Jenny?... Oh, I...well, it *is* blocked. That is, it *was*. I came back this morning to see if I could clear some of it and it wasn't as bad as I thought... Look, you two, how did you find the other entrance?'

'A cat,' Adam said. 'A cat led us here. We'll explain about that later.'

'Oh, well...' Martin licked his lips again. 'I had to be sure. I mean, you might have been in this with Guy.'

'Both of us?' Adam said sceptically.

Martin took a deep breath. 'Look, I'll tell you the truth. I had to make sure about you. I mean, when I heard you coming I thought you were Guy. I thought you must have known about the tunnel all along. And I had to be careful. You see, I've found something down here.' He pointed with the torch. 'Down there, towards the cave. You take a look for yourself.'

I saw Adam frown as he brushed past my cousin, then he was a black shape in front of me, the torchlight wavering along the left-hand branch of the tunnel, which sloped steeply downwards. He paused, with an indrawn breath, and drew aside to let me see what lay there.

Four large brown suitcases, two of them strapped up. The other two lay open on the tunnel floor. One of them contained the butts and barrels of some kind of rifle. The other was full of boxes of ammunition.

Adam knelt down to examine the guns, muttering imprecations, and I heard Martin come up behind me. Squeezing into the space beside me, he said, 'I opened them to see what they were. Guy's really up to his neck, isn't he?'

Very slowly, Adam lifted his head, shadows shifting on his angular face.

'Yes,' he said quietly. 'Tell me, Martin—how do you suppose Guy found these tunnels? Jonathon searched for years. You looked. Lyn and I looked. None of us found anything. But a total stranger walks in and makes use of the system right away. Now how do you explain that?'

'I don't.' Suddenly Martin's voice was flat. He put his hand on my back and thrust me towards Adam, making me stumble into him. When I looked round, Martin had both his torch and one of the rifles trained on us.

CHAPTER TWELVE

'Drop your torch,' Martin commanded. 'Drop it, Adam, or I'll use this rifle.'

The rubber torch fell from Adam's hand, its glass up against one of the cases. Now we couldn't see Martin clearly, just the bright light in our eyes and the shining barrel of the rifle he held so steadily. He backed away, stopping just beyond the junction of the tunnels, in the branch which led to the Mount.

'Now come,' he ordered. 'Lyn first. No...don't bend down, Adam. Just walk slowly. Back the way you came.'

I hesitated nervously, in the black mouth of the long tunnel. Adam was close behind me. Suddenly he threw me to one side, into the darkness. I had an impression of him hurling himself forwards. There was a deafening report as the rifle went off. Martin's torch rolled, shadows tilting crazily. And then the thunder began.

Only it wasn't thunder. It was the rock above us protesting at the noise. I think I screamed.

Martin appeared. He snatched up his torch and flashed it at me, jerking the rifle.

'Get going!'

'Adam!' I cried. 'Where is he? You can't...'

Martin rushed at me and grabbed me, pushing me ahead of him. 'Damn you, Lyn. Move it! Move! This whole bloody place...'

We ran a few yards. Behind us the rumbling turned into a roar and then a grinding crash that shook the ground behind us. Martin swung me round, holding me with the rifle cold under my chin and the torch directed back the way we had come. The tunnel was really blocked now. Some of the loose fragments still rolled on the floor. The air was full of choking dust.

Adam...

Before the noise had stopped, it started again. Except that this time it was from the other direction, all around us. On reflex, I crouched down with my arms over my head, waiting for the deluge. It came again, the roaring crash of collapsing rock. Something banged against my ankle. I heard Martin yell. Then I was coughing, retching, with the blinding dust in my eyes, filling my throat.

The torch rested by my feet, showing me the dust swirling like mist. Through it, I saw Martin lying on his face a few feet away. There was blood on the cheek I could see and his eyes were closed. As the dust cleared further, I saw that one of his legs was pinioned under a huge boulder. The main fall had just missed him.

Scrambling unsteadily to my feet, throat sore and eyes streaming, I bent over my cousin. He was still breathing, but we were both trapped in an enclosed cave some ten feet long by three wide by six high. Martin was covered in dust. It caked the blood on his face, whitened his hair and eyelashes...his eyes fluttered open. He murmured, 'My leg! Oh, God, my leg!'

I couldn't shift the boulder by pulling it. I sat down, my back braced against the wall, my legs across Martin's uninjured one, my feet up on the big rock. And I pushed. The strain ripped through my thighs and back, constricted my chest. But the boulder moved. Another ounce of effort—all I had left—and it rocked away. I snatched Martin's leg out of the way. His jeans were bloody. He screamed with pain. But when the boulder came back to rest he was free of it.

He had passed out again. I set the torch so that I could see his leg, my hands sticky with his blood. I couldn't tear the faded denim of his jeans.

My eye fell on the rifle lying by Martin's outflung hand. It was all I had for use as a splint. And for bandages... I pulled off my filthy jumper and sleeveless blouse, tearing the blouse into wide strips. While Martin was still unconscious, I got him onto his back and placed the rifle beside his injured leg, barrel downwards, tying it tightly in place. The blouse wasn't enough, so I set to work on Martin, stripping off his sweater and blue shirt, adding lengths from the shirt to the orange bindings already in place. My one consolation was that he had stopped bleeding. If he had damaged an artery there would have been little I could do.

The patchy first aid took me a long time and when I had finished I was sweating profusely, on the verge of exhaustion, and wondering how long the air would last. I sat with my head down, trying to gather my strength.

'Lyn.' Martin's hoarse voice roused me. 'What's the time?'

'Nearly twelve.'

'How long have we...'

'About three quarters of an hour, as far as I can tell. I'm going to start digging in a minute.'

'I shouldn't bother,' Martin said dully. 'Didn't you hear it? There must be tons of it. Both ways.'

'I don't intend to sit here and wait,' I returned, scrambling to my feet.

He raised himself on his elbows, staring down at his naked, glistening chest and the odd mixture of bandages on his leg. A crooked smile grotesquely lit his face.

'Thanks. Your blouse, I presume? You look very fetching half-naked, but why did you bother?'

'I want to be sure you're fit to face the police,' I said, swiftly pulling on the dust-filled jumper I had discarded. He was powerless, but I didn't like the way he looked at me.

Wincing with pain, Martin dragged

himself across the rock floor until he was sitting with his back propped against the wall. I turned away from him and began to pry at the rocks near the top of the tunnel.

'Adam made me do it,' Martin said. 'I didn't intend to shoot him.'

Adam. It was odd, but I was too numb to feel anything. Shock had taken over. Adam must be dead. Either Martin had killed him, or the rock fall. My sole reason for trying to get out of this prison was to make sure the world knew what Martin had done.

'Don't you want to know how all this started?' Martin asked. 'Lyn, don't waste your energy. You'll never move those rocks... Oh, all right. Break your nails. Nobody'll ever see them again. We aren't going to be found. Ever.'

I ignored him, though he seemed to be right. My fingers were already sore and I hadn't moved one single rock. They were either too big or too tightly jammed.

'I wonder what'll happen to those guns?' he said rhetorically, and gave a sharp laugh. 'They won't do the IRA any good, anyway.'

'The IRA?' I repeated, turning to stare at him.

'Yes, Lynda dear. Your cousin Martin got himself involved in arms smuggling. Doesn't that amuse you?'

I walked past him, climbing onto the blockage the other side and beginning another vain attempt to dislodge something.

'You'll never guess who else was in it with me.' His voice taunted me. 'Never in a million years. Go on. Have a guess.'

'I'm in no mood for guessing games,' I said tartly.

'I'll tell you then—Uncle Jonathon!... Ah, I knew that would make you prick your ears up.'

I leapt down from my perch, clenching my sticky, dirty hands. 'You liar, Martin!'

'Why should I lie? This is a death-bed confession. It would be more friendly if you came and sat by me. Spend our last hours alone together.'

'I'd rather sit near a tarantula!' I spat, hating him.

'But are you going to listen?'

'I don't have much choice.' I rested on the boulder which had broken his leg, my hands raw, the finger-ends beginning to bleed. 'But if you tell me any more lies about Uncle Jonathon I swear I'll hit you.'

'No lies,' Martin said. 'The truth. But I'm afraid it will have to be about Uncle Jonathon. He was the one who started it.' He paused, watching me with eyes that glittered in the torchlight. 'He found the tunnel years ago,' he said eventually. 'Aunt Maude showed him the secret stairs and he found the way to the cave and to your Gran's cottage. The tunnel used to come out in the cellar at the cottage, but it had been bricked up and part of it had fallen in, leaving that hole in the Wilderness... You can imagine what it meant to Uncle Jonathon. Everybody looked down on him. He was the younger brother, deaf and crippled, with a stupid obsession everybody scoffed at. So he decided to do something very daring. He started bringing in cigarettes and brandy, with the help of a chap from Ilfracombe, who had a yacht. The yacht would anchor in the cove at night, transfer the stuff by rowing boat to Uncle Jonathon, who stowed it in the tunnels until he could dispose of it.'

'You ought to be a writer,' I said

disgustedly. 'Uncle Jonathon wouldn't have asked me to look for the tunnel if he'd known...'

'No, wait, wait,' Martin interrupted. 'I'm coming to that... There he was, year after year, dealing in trifling things and thinking he was a big man. Then, three years ago, I found out about it. I saw the rowing boat come in one night and went down to investigate. So I was cut in. It was no skin off my teeth and a few extra pounds came in handy...

'I got to know the son of this chap with the yacht and through him I met an Italian who had a nice line in bringing immigrants through back doors. A pretty close watch is kept on the East coast but on this side of the country they don't expect it. Not that it was many. Three or four each time. But it made extra profits. Those chaps will pay anything to get here. The trouble was, Uncle Jonathon wasn't too keen. He took a lot of persuading.' He paused, running his tongue round his lips. 'I fancy a nice cool beer.'

'All we've got is a dusty puddle,' I said with some satisfaction, enjoying his discomfiture. 'Now you can guess how that poor man felt. That poor sick man who you brought through and left to die.'

'I didn't know!' Martin denied angrily. 'They told me he was suffering from sea-sickness. It was dark. I didn't bother to examine him. And anyway there were three others with him. They were the ones who abandoned him. It's not my responsibility.'

'Oh, you're...despicable! I suppose you were my poltergeist, too. And Gran...' I stopped, feeling sick.

'That was unfortunate,' Martin growled. 'I didn't intend her any harm. It was that bloody dog. It must have been sleeping in the greenhouse, with the door open. It came rushing out when it heard us, making one hell of a row. I saw the kitchen light go on just as the stupid dog got through the fence, so I grabbed him and shut him up.' His hands made graphic gestures in the air. 'Then your Gran came out. She shouted, "Smokey, Smokey," twice and suddenly put her hand to her chest and collapsed. It was pouring with rain and I knew she'd get soaked, so I flung the dog over into the churchyard and climbed the fence to help your Gran. I was taking quite a risk.'

'Big of you,' I muttered disgustedly.

'I took her to shelter, in the greenhouse, and was thinking about calling you when I realised she was dead. It was too late for anyone to do anything. So I ran. It was the only thing I could do... Uncle Jonathon guessed that I'd had something to do with it and he was furious. He wanted to call a halt to our operations. That's why he asked you to look for the tunnel. He was hoping you'd find it and tell everyone, so that I'd have to stop the smuggling. I had no idea what he was up to until that day I brought him home from hospital. From what you said, I guessed a little. Uncle Jonathon told me the rest. So I went down to the cave and camouflaged the tunnel entrance. It's difficult enough to find when you know where it is, but I wasn't taking any chances. And you and Adam didn't look very hard.

'Anyway, while Uncle Jonathon was in hospital, I had a call from my Italian friend. There was a shipment of guns coming through. Something had gone wrong with the usual arrangements and he wanted them taken from our cove. He knew they'd be safe hidden in the tunnels until the ship arrived. But I couldn't risk taking them through with you in the cottage, so I had to get you away. I know you believe in the supernatural. So I started the ghost scare. I tape-recorded a terrier they've got out at one of the farms. And when that didn't work I had to go further. It wasn't only me this time, you see. There were two men coming to check on where the guns were left. If you'd heard us and come out...I was worried about you, Lyn.

'But I was fool enough to tell Uncle Jonathon about the guns. He need never have known they were coming. It was ages since he'd been in the tunnels himself. He'd been leaving it to me. And after I told him he said I'd never get away with it. He said he'd stop me. So I kept a close eye on him. I saw him go to Aunt Maude's room that night and heard him tell her he was going to shut off the tunnels so that she needn't be afraid of someone getting in. And he went down the stairs.

'I left the house and went down to the cove and found him bashing away at the tunnel entrance with a hammer, trying to fetch enough rock down to block it for good. He'd probably have got himself killed if I hadn't caught him at it. Maybe that's what he wanted. He said, "All right, Martin. I've had enough. I can't take any more," and he left the cave and started up the cliff path. I'd forgotten about his vertigo. I was too far away to do anything. He was reeling like a drunkard and slipped. The edge gave way. The tide was full. He was swept out with the undertow and I never saw him again.

'I had to carry on as if I knew nothing. I could never have explained how I came to be there when he fell. But it *was* an accident. You've got to believe that, Lyn.'

'It suited your purpose, though,' I said. 'With Uncle Jonathon out of the way... When did you find out that *I* knew about the secret stairs?'

'Last night—when Jenny asked me to help her. The safest thing I could do was go along with her, but tell her the tunnel was blocked. That's what I was trying to do this morning—block it. That's why I'd got the gun loaded. I planned to start a cave-in that would cut off the branch leading to the stairs. And then I heard *you* coming. I was trying to bluff my way out, trying to implicate Guy, like I did yesterday when we talked to those yobbos. But Adam was too sharp for his own good.'

'And what did you plan to do with us?'

'I don't know. I hadn't thought that far. Maybe tie you up and leave you until the guns were gone—they're coming for them tonight, but I don't know what they'll do now. I shan't be there to deliver.'

'Someone will be, if I know anything. Those friends of yours are in for a shock. Adam went to the police this morning and told them everything we knew. They'll be watching the cove...it was you that hit Adam that night, wasn't it? Hit him and then dragged him back to the stairs, and smeared his blood on the beam.'

'It was his own fault,' Martin said. 'Just the very night when the guns were coming, he decides to play hero... I thought the blood on the beam would confuse the issue long enough for me to get rid of the guns. It was sheer luck that he forgot what had really happened. I hadn't counted on that.'

'What a pity your luck didn't last,' I said. 'Who shall you curse with your dying breath? Your Italian friend? What's his name?'

'Guiseppe. But he calls himself Joe. Peter never did tell me his second name.'

'Peter?'

'The one with the yacht.'

'Peter who?' I asked.

Martin sighed. 'What does it matter? You'll never meet him now. Pity. You'd like him.'

'He sounds just my type,' I said with sarcasm. 'But who knows? I may meet him yet. Haven't you noticed that it's warm in here, but not getting stuffy?'

'We shan't notice it yet,' he said. 'It takes hours.'

'Does it? I wouldn't know about that. But when I was up near the ceiling a while ago I felt a cool draught on my hands. How deep under the ground do you suppose we are?'

Martin's face contorted with fury as he realised why I had sat so calmly and let him talk. His muscular shoulders jerked, as if he would have liked to grab me. Turning away from him, I climbed up on the rockfall until I felt again the fresh air coming in. I fastened my sore fingers round the rock nearest to the flow and tugged at it sharply. It came away, taking me with it, so that I fell to the floor, bombarded by bouncing rocks. I lay flat, my arms over my head.

'You bloody fool!' Martin exclaimed in terror. 'We'll both be crushed.'

When the slip subsided, I sat up and examined with interest the scattering of dark earth which had come down with the rocks. And when I looked up at the top of the pile I saw a faint light showing.

'Daylight!' Martin said incredulously. 'Lyn!'

'Yes, I know.' I got up, gingerly testing my limbs. I was filthy, cut and bruised, aching in every muscle, but I wasn't done yet.

A lot of earth had come down. It lay in dark patches over the dusty rocks and floor. The ground above must have subsided. Once more I climbed onto the pile of rocks, reaching to the top, where the daylight showed. The rubble there was loose now and I worked feverishly, throwing rocks behind me one at a time. Martin had retreated into the far corner to watch me sullenly, but he was the least of my worries now. He was immobilised and the gun was unusable.

Clumps of earth rained down on my face as the space grew bigger, the light brighter. I could see the grey sky and the brightness where the sun was trying to come through.

'I think I can manage to get out now,' I

panted eventually. 'I'll get help at once.'

Martin's voice came to me. 'You needn't tell the truth. I'll make it worth your while.'

I turned round for one last time, sickened by him. 'After what you've done? To Gran. To Uncle Jonathon. To Adam...' My throat closed up and I began to climb, ignoring the pain in my hands and arms.

My head emerged in a shallow depression where a gorse bush was tilting down the slope. I got one arm through, then my shoulders. The other arm...

The Mount was about a hundred yards away. I saw two policemen standing on the clifftop, looking down into the cove.

My legs came free and I stood up, staggering towards the men, shouting, 'Hey! Hey! Over here!'

And then I saw the group standing on the terrace. Jenny was there. And Melly, with Uncle James and Guy.

I began to run towards them and stopped as a voice called my name from the edge of the cliff.

It was Adam. He was limping slightly and there was dried blood on his slacks around a rent in the material above his knee. But he was alive. Not buried under tons of...

'Adam!' I collapsed into his arms, weeping with joy. 'Adam, darling!'

He held me tight against him, his head bent to mine, but he didn't say anything. He let the nearness of his body tell me all I needed to know.

'Where's Martin?' Uncle James' voice said, and I turned my head to look at him, seeing him pale and trembling.

'He's down where I was. His leg's broken. You'll need ropes to get him out.'

My uncle stumped away and the group of policemen dispersed, concentrating for the moment on rescuing Martin.

'Did Martin talk to you?' Jenny asked. 'Was he responsible for...'

'Of course he wasn't!' Melly cried, face flaming, her brimming eyes fixed accusingly on Adam. 'It's all a mistake. Adam's wrong! Wrong!'

'Well, it wouldn't surprise *me*,' Jenny said. 'I've always thought Martin was too big for his boots. He was bound to over-reach himself sooner or later.'

Melly was beside herself with worry, fear and anger. She was spluttering impotently,

'Oh...you...' when Guy stepped forward, his handsome face dark as thunder, and gently put his arm round her.

'We've had about enough of your opinions!' he said forcibly, making Jenny start and step away. Guy bent over Melly with surprising tenderness. 'Come on. Let's go and see if we can help.'

They moved away, Melly leaning on Guy and weeping. Jenny's cheeks were flushed as she turned back to me.

'Well? Did he tell you anything?'

'Yes,' I said, and rubbed my face on Adam's dusty sweater, knowing that I could never tell Jenny that her father had also been deeply involved. She would find out eventually, but not from me. Jenny wasn't the only one who was going to be hurt.

'Oh, well,' she said carelessly. 'Since you're the heroine of the hour I don't suppose I shall be needed. I think I'll go and ring Grant and tell him I'm coming back right away. There doesn't seem to be any point in my staying now.'

'No point at all,' Adam replied, his arm still warmly around me.

From the corner of my eye I saw Jenny toss her head as she turned away.

'I thought I'd lost you,' Adam said into my hair.

'I thought the same,' I said, shivering. 'I thought Martin had killed you.'

'The shot grazed my thigh, that's all. And he sent me flying. Before I could collect myself, I had to dodge away from the rockfall. I was sure it must have landed on you and Martin. I got out through the cave and phoned the police from the Mount. I tried the other end of the tunnel, but there must have been several falls. I couldn't get more than a few yards down there. It's been balanced precariously all these years... Oh, Lyn, I've been nearly out of my mind!' He looked up at the heavy layer of cloud. 'It's starting to rain. Shall we go back to the cottage?'

'Oh yes,' I breathed. 'Yes, let's go home.'

This Large Print Book for the Partially sighted, who cannot read normal print, is published under the auspices of

THE ULVERSCROFT FOUNDATION

THE ULVERSCROFT FOUNDATION

. . . we hope that you have enjoyed this Large Print Book. Please think for a moment about those people who have worse eyesight problems than you . . . and are unable to even read or enjoy Large Print, without great difficulty.

You can help them by sending a donation, large or small to:

The Ulverscroft Foundation,
1, The Green, Bradgate Road,
Anstey, Leicestershire, LE7 7FU,
England.

or request a copy of our brochure for more details.

The Foundation will use all your help to assist those people who are handicapped by various sight problems and need special attention.

Thank you very much for your help.